Like a

Dance

DELIA LATHAM

TABLE OF CONTENTS

Published by Heaven's Touch Books
First Edition, 2019
Published in the United States of America

ISBN: 978-1799121299

Contact information:
Delia Latham: **delia@delialatham.net**

Dear Reader,

Has anyone ever asked you for help, and then refused to allow you to do anything...or simply vetoed your every suggestion? It's frustrating, isn't it? Especially when you see changes that need to be made, or can think of fifty different ways in which your friend could improve her situation.

And yet, we do that to our Savior—Who sees our past, our present and our future. He *knows* exactly what we need, when we need it, and how to make it happen...but He awaits our plea for assistance. Maybe we've already asked for His help, and now He's waiting for us to actually *let Him do what we asked Him to do!*

The heroine in *Like a Dance* is the queen of holding onto problems she should have released to Christ a long time ago. She loves God. She trusts Him. But she has a problem with surrendering...releasing...letting go and letting God (especially where her little girl is concerned).

I get it. Do you? Yet when we insist on maintaining control, rather than handing over the reins to Christ, we miss out on so much. God's ways are always better than ours. His answer is always the best answer. He. Is. God. He knows how to make everything perfect.

My goal in the here-and-now is to work on letting God be God...trusting Him with my life, my love, my home, my heart...my everything. Will you join me? Let's do this together, shall we?

I look forward to hearing about how God moves for you when you let Him lead your dance of life.

Dedication

~ In Memory of Sister Loretta Copus ~

The sweetest, most dedicated prayer warrior
I've ever known, Sis. Copus often danced while she
prayed, and she often prayed in a language unknown
to me, but which I thought of as Native American.
She was an incredible role model and mentor,
and taught me so much about Christ…about life…
about love…about prayer. In all the years I knew
this beautiful lady, I never once heard her say
a harsh word about a single soul. I never saw her
behave in an impatient manner with anyone,
even those who most deserved it. She was a
shining example of Christ-likeness. I loved her
from the bottom of my heart, and will never,
ever forget her.

I can see you dancing and singing
in the midst of an entire flock of heavenly
hummingbirds, Sis. Copus…and I believe Jesus Christ
Himself is your dance partner.

Key Verse

A man's heart plans his way,
but the LORD directs his steps.

~ Proverbs 16:9 (NKJV) ~

Chapter 1

AWED, AMAZED, AND UTTERLY SPEECHLESS, Teela Vincent didn't even breathe.

She sat alone at a table for two. Half a dozen or so various-sized tables surrounded her, all occupied. The little group filled the dining room of a wonderful old bed and breakfast nestled into the lush greenness of an Arkansas hollow.

Hummingbird Hollow, to be precise. And in this moment, Teela saw how it got its name.

Outside the sliding glass doors, a trio of hummingbirds flitted and zoomed around a small feeder attached to the glass. Their vivid colors shone in the sunlight—one with a deep red throat, another sporting bright blue wings. Pure white feathers glistened and dazzled on the third hummer.

The blue one tapped at the glass. Three tiny pecks of his long beak elicited gasps and soft exclamations from the humans inside, including Teela—who'd been certain she couldn't make a sound at all.

She smiled when a lovely Native American woman stopped to fill her water glass. Toni Littlebird owned the bed and breakfast, which she called Inn the Hollow. She'd told Teela that a grandfather of many generations past had built the structure. To make his beloved Cherokee wife feel more at home away from her people, he'd designed it to resemble a tribal meeting house. But the building took on a drastically altered appearance as later generations added on—a room here and there, in first one direction and then another. The home might never grace the cover of *House Beautiful*, but it possessed something far better than classic beauty—a warmth, a hominess that called to Teela's heart and soul and made her want to stay forever.

"Meet my friends." Toni pointed her chin toward the window. "Sapphire is my little blue love. Ruby Bright is the red-throated one. And the white beauty—the albino—that's Diamond."

"They're stunning! I didn't know it was possible to domesticate hummingbirds."

"Stunning they are, but they are not domesticated...and certainly not pets. They're my friends. Perhaps my closest ones. God gives us such lovely gifts, doesn't He?" Toni moved on to the next table, pretty smile in place and water pitcher ready to pour.

Sapphire lifted and hovered above the feeder. He cocked his tiny head both ways to take in the dinner scene inside the house, then tapped the glass again—twice this time.

With all eyes turned to the window, the birds lifted as if on cue and dipped their tiny bodies to one side and then the other, in perfect synchrony. Then, having charmed and mesmerized their small audience, they darted off into the garden—beautiful wings ablaze with sunshine. As they flew, they continued the display of graceful movement. Ruby Bright hovered in place while Diamond and Sapphire circled him from above and below. The speed at which they zoomed around their friend turned their circular movement into a blur of bright red and blue.

Then the three little showoffs rose a little higher into the air, where they were joined by several other hummers. The entire group formed into…Teela gaped. *Is this real? A perfect infinity symbol.* The moving shape shimmered with color that reflected off tiny wings in glistening sun sparkles.

Teela gasped, and one hand flew up to rest on her heart. "Oh…!" she breathed. "It's like a dance!"

She thought she'd uttered a mere whisper, and yet a male diner seated across the room looked up in response—and straight into her soul. Gorgeous bone structure. Deep, velvet brown eyes. Overall quite easy on the eyes. A smile lifted one corner of finely drawn lips, and he offered a slight, gentlemanly nod.

Teela caught her breath. Her cheeks warmed. She returned the nod, then tore her gaze from the stranger's and back to the window.

But the hummingbird show had ended. The wee performers had disappeared into the gardens.

A sigh escaped. She couldn't help it.

She'd seen hummingbirds before. She'd watched them flit around feeders, and laughed at their silly, territorial way of chasing off competition for the sweet nectar they so loved. But she'd never witnessed such an amazing display of deliberate performance.…such a beautiful, graceful dance. Almost as if it had been expertly choreographed. As a former professional dancer, she appreciated the beauty and perfection of the tiny creatures' dance routine.

How was such a thing even possible?

"May I sit with you for a moment?"

Caught up in her thoughts, she hadn't noticed the handsome stranger approaching her table. Now he stood beside her, soft brown eyes fixed on her face, one dark eyebrow lifted in inquiry.

"Yes, of course. Please join me."

Her visitor took the seat across from her without looking

away for even an instant.

"Thank you. I'm Booth Meadows."

"Booth…I like that. I'm—"

"Wait. Allow me. You are Teela Vincent."

Taken aback for a moment, she paused before offering a little dip of her chin. "I am." She probably knew where he got that information, but she asked anyway. "And you know this because…?"

"I watched an entire season of *Save A Dance for Me*—and not because I'm a fan of the show. I happened on it one night while channel surfing. The first thing I saw was your gorgeous face, and I couldn't move on to save my life. You fascinated me. I watched every episode for the rest of the season—just so I could see you dance." He shook his head, his gaze unwavering. "But the next season, you were gone. I tried to find information online…" He chuckled and lowered his head for an instant. "Believe me, I tried. But there was nothing. You'd simply disappeared, and I thought I'd never see you again. But here you are at Hummingbird Hollow, as if you walked right out of my dreams."

Teela caught her breath. Any other time, from any other man, that little speech would have terrified her. But Booth Meadows was no stalker. She'd always possessed a keen sense of character, or its lack, in others. Besides, her heart simply refused to believe such a thing about this man.

She managed a soft burst of laughter. "I assure you, I'm quite real, and truly flattered. Thank you for making my day in such a sweet manner."

"Oh, trust me—I'm not a flatterer. I speak the truth or nothing at all. You are incredibly talented, Teela…and I can't even find words to describe your beauty. I think God must've gotten a little mixed up and sent an angel to earth." He cleared his throat, and his lips curved into a crooked smile. Teela

4

gathered he wasn't practiced at being charming. "You don't happen to have a pair of invisible wings, do you?"

Now Teela's laughter came a little more easily. "I refuse to answer on the grounds that a girl's gotta have a little mystery about her…don't you think?"

"You have more than your share of that." Booth's dark eyebrows drew together. His head tilted slightly to the side. "Where did you disappear to, Teela Vincent? Oh, I know! You were called back to Heaven to be fitted for new wings." He smiled. "Or was it a halo?"

Booth couldn't believe his own audacity. Teela would've been totally justified had she ordered him away from her table…or stood and walked out of the room.

Yet there she still sat. Her smile seemed a little shy, but she didn't look poised to fly away. On the other hand, her slightly timid smile wavered a bit at his question.

"No, I haven't been there recently, but—" She broke off, and Booth noted the slight change of color in her cheeks when she paled.

"But someone you loved made that one-way trip." He spoke gently, somehow knowing in his heart that he was right.

"Yes." She drew a deep breath and lowered her gaze.

Booth said nothing, giving her a moment.

After a short beat, she lifted her chin and stiffened her shoulders, visibly taking on strength to continue.

"My best friend since childhood. I never had any siblings, but I considered Annalise a sister. We were close…really close, from kindergarten on. She was an only child too. Never knew her father, and lost her mother to cancer while we were in college. We were roommates, and then, after graduation, we rented a small house together. The two of us really were inseparable." She pulled in a breath. "One day a couple of years ago, Annalise was sitting at a red light on her way home from work. She was a nurse…a good one who cared deeply about her patients. She always took the same route home, specifically because it never had a lot of traffic. It didn't have much that day either…but as she sat at that signal light, a car traveling at close to a hundred miles an hour rammed her from behind. The driver was some big drug trafficker, trying to evade the police on his tail. Annalise–" Teela paused. Cleared her throat. "She died on the scene."

"Oh, no." Booth desperately wanted to take her hand, but feared she'd think him presumptuous. "That's…hard. I'm sorry."

"Thank you. I was devastated, but the one hurt most by Annalise's death was…" She raised a pair of translucent blue eyes, misty with unshed tears. "Her baby girl. Kinsley was only eight weeks old."

Booth blanched. "That's terrible. No one ever realizes how far the consequences of these tragedies can reach." He shook his head, almost physically attuned to Teela's pain. "Where is the child now?"

"Annalise had no family, and the child's father made it clear from the start that he never wanted anything to do with either of them. We agreed early in her pregnancy that I would take the child should anything ever happen to her. All the paperwork was signed, filed, and in order." She smiled through the tears brimming in her eyes. "Upon Annalise's death, I became a mommy. I knew I couldn't deal with the rigid schedule of the show and still give Kinsley the attention she deserved. So I made a choice—one I've never regretted. She's my life."

Booth sat, stunned and speechless.

This gorgeous woman didn't have wings or a halo, but she must be an angel. She hadn't made a trip to Heaven, but her friend had, and now Teela had a daughter. A little girl.

Booth hadn't a chance of pursuing a relationship with her, even though he'd been half in love with Teela ever since he first saw her glide across the screen as one of the pros on a dance competition television series. When he'd looked up in response to her breathless statement mere moments ago—"It's like a dance!"—and realized she was the woman of his dreams, his heart had missed a beat. And then another.

Off screen—up close and without the overdone cosmetics and flash of the show—Teela's beauty was almost heartbreaking. Ethereal. Unreal. Having met her, Booth might forevermore be blind to other women.

"Hey, Booth!" His friend Cass called out from across the room. "We're making a quick trip into Eureka Springs. Want to come?"

"I…uhm…"

Teela smiled. "It was nice chatting with you, Booth and I apologize for unloading on you like that." She shook her head. "I don't usually share so freely, even with people I know."

"I'm glad you did this time." He glanced across the room, where Cass stood with a little group of friends, including her new fiancé, Ryder. "I'd like to stay and talk, but…"

"Go with your friends. I need to get back upstairs anyway. Being away from Kinsley is so hard. I left her with my pastor's wife, and I trust her—I really do, implicitly—but I miss my baby so much! I've got to call and check on her, for at least the tenth time today." She laughed softly, and folded her napkin as she stood. "Who knows? We may meet again. Goodbye for now, Booth Meadows."

"Until later, Teela Vincent."

He watched her walk upstairs before joining Cass and the others.

This was best. Just a simple goodbye, before he lost any more of his heart. No matter how much he wanted to know her better, a relationship with Teela was out of the question,.

Booth couldn't be a father, not to his own children, not to someone else's. Not now…not ever.

Chapter 2

Six months later.

TEELA USED A LARGE TURNKEY to unlock her suite at Hummingbird Hollow.

"Mommy, Mommy!" A tiny bundle of pure energy slammed into her legs and held on tight. "I wake up, see? Cahla say you be back *weoh* soon." She swung toward a large, plain woman standing near the window. "See, Cahla, Mommy's back wight now. See?"

Carla chuckled. "I see, little one. Mommy's back right now, and Carla's off to help Chef Jonathan in the kitchen." She offered Teela a kind smile. "She's a sweetheart, Miss Teela. Woke up in the sweetest mood, and not a single tear at finding herself alone with a stranger."

"You were so sweet to stay with her. I appreciate your time and your kindness."

Carla patted her shoulder. "It was my pleasure, dear. Children are the most joyful and pure of all God's creations. I enjoy any time I can spend with them. God didn't see fit to give me my own, so I consider them all mine, and time spent with little ones makes any day special." She picked up Kinsley and nuzzled her hair. "Maybe Mommy will let me stay with you again while you're here. Would that be okay with you, little miss?"

"Yep. I like Cahla."

"Well, then. The boss has spoken." Carla set her gently on her feet. "Shall I send something up for her dinner, Miss Teela?"

"That would be lovely. And please, I'd be honored if you'd just call me Teela."

"Teela it is then." She winked at Kinsley. "Someone will be up lickety-split with your dinner."

"Bye, Cahla." As the door closed behind the kindly woman, the child reached for Teela, who picked her up and cuddled her close, breathing in the delightful aroma of bubble bath and clean toddler. "I hungwy, Mommy."

"I know, darling. Carla will send your dinner up right away. Did you have fun while I was gone?"

Kinsley's tiny chin bounced up and down, sending silky black hair swinging around her shoulders and against her face. She absently brushed it back with one pudgy hand. "Cahla played patty-cake with me. And hide awound the wosie."

Teela bit back a chuckle. Kinsley couldn't seem to separate hide-and-go-seek and Ring Around the Rosie. Someday soon, she'd outgrow that little foible. Her heart pinched at the thought. In the meantime, she stored it away as a precious, beloved memory to share with her daughter later in life.

"Oh, that's nice! I think she might've let you play in the bathtub too. You smell oh-so-clean and sweet!"

Kinsley giggled. "Cahla gave me *extwa* bubbles, and she put some in my hayoh too." She stuck her head against Teela's chin. "See? Sniff, Mommy."

Teela grinned and made a big show of smelling the shiny tresses. "Mmmmm, nice!"

Barely past her third birthday, Kinsley possessed an impressive vocabulary, but still had a bit of a problem pronouncing her r's. Even so, she'd been deemed "one-hundred-percent healthy and two-hundred-percent precocious" by her doctor, who assured Teela she had nothing to worry about. "She'll be speaking clear as day before you even know it, Miss Vincent. Just do what you've been doing and let Kinsley do the same. These things tend to happen when they're supposed to."

As long as she knew Kinsley's broad r's were not unusual at her age, Teela had no problem with them. In all truth, she found the child's current manner of speech quite adorable, and knowing it wouldn't last long saddened her a bit. Children grew up far too quickly. Hadn't it been only a few days ago that she and Annalise brought a newborn baby home from the hospital? And just look at her now.

"Mommy, how come we not seepin' at home. Huh? I 'pos'a seep in my pwincess bed!"

"I know, sweet girl, and we won't be away for too very long. I have to get back for my classes, 'cause Miss Mellie can only help out for a little while. But Mommy wanted some time just for you and me, that's why we're here." She widened her eyes and put all the excitement she knew how into her expression. "Guess where we're going tomorrow?"

Kinsley frowned. "Whayow?

"We're going to see some lions and tigers and bears...oh, my!"

Big green eyes rounded. "We *ahh*?" A little shiver shook her tiny frame. "Will they eat me?"

Teela chuckled. "No, my darling. They won't eat you. They'll be on the other side of a very strong fence, but you can see them, and see how they live. Would you like that?"

The child nodded.

"Then off to see the lions and tigers and bears we go. Oh!" She turned to answer a light tap on the door. "That must be your dinner."

Moments later, she set Kinsley up at the vanity with her plate and a cup of milk. "You eat while I change clothes, okay?"

"Okay, Mommy. I a big gowul. I can eat all by myself."

"I know. I'm so proud of my big girl."

As she changed into comfortable clothing for the evening, she thought about the last time she'd visited this lovely bed and breakfast, Inn the Hollow. She'd come to Eureka Springs, Arkansas to take advantage of a one-of-a-kind, once-in-a-lifetime dancing class with a renowned ballroom dancer. While she no longer danced professionally, she taught others to dance, and made a point to stay abreast of dancing techniques, moves and methods. During that visit, she'd had next to no time to really appreciate the gorgeous, lush green surroundings, and had determined to come back when she could stay longer.

But since she tried to always be completely honest, she had to admit it was another memory of that previous visit that haunted her dreams at night.

There'd been some scary moments in a glass chapel in the woods, praying for a couple trapped in a nearby cave with an angry mama bear. But that wasn't what she dreamed about. Not that…and certainly not the excellent dance class. Nor did the charming, artsy little town of Eureka Springs show up in her dream world. Not even this wonderful, homey bed and breakfast that seemed to be a mecca of sorts for hummingbirds of all kinds, colors and species. None of those things made their way into her sleeping conscience and solidified her need to return to Hummingbird Hollow.

Her sleep and her life had been haunted for the past few months by a man.

She'd met Booth Meadows only once, and the encounter had been all too brief. Yet ever since, she kept expecting to see him around every corner, looked for him in every stranger she passed on the street…and met with him in her dreams.

Every. Single. Night.

Such a gentleman! Something about him had reached out to her, took hold of her imagination…her emotions…her senses. If Teela had any intention of getting involved with a man, she certainly wouldn't mind seeing more of that one.

Of course, she had no such intention, and running into Booth again wasn't likely to happen. Not in a million years.

But if she walked downstairs tomorrow and found him sitting at the table where they'd visited so briefly… If he happened to invite her to share that table… If circumstances permitted them to hang out together for a short time… Well, she'd just have to make sure he understood that any time they spent together would be nothing more than a way to pass a few moments of time, because she couldn't get serious about Booth. Where did he even live? She had no idea who he was or what he did. None of that really mattered anyway. The simple truth was, she couldn't allow any man into her life, not on a serious level.

Right now, and for many years into the future, she was dedicated to being Kinsley's mommy. Back home in a suburb of Sugar Land, Texas, she was also a ballroom dance instructor, and the praise dance leader at church. Her life was full to the brim with busyness. No time remained for love and romance.

"Mommy?" Her daughter's sweet voice broke into her reverie. "Will you wead to me now?"

"I'll be right there, Kinny Kat."

Dressed in comfortable sweats, with her long hair released from its customary messy bun and spilling around her shoulders, she gathered up the remains of Kinsley's dinner and set it on a side table. A staff member would most likely be up to claim it before long.

"In my lap? Or shall we lie on the bed?"

In answer, Kinsley pointed to a big rocking chair beside the window. This time of night, only darkness lay beyond the glass pane. But somehow, even that seemed soothing while safely ensconced in this huge, old Native American home. Teela settled into the rocker and Kinsley, book in hand, scrambled up onto her lap.

I'll Love You Forever—a touching, unforgettable tale by Robert Munsch—had become her daughter's favorite of the many books in her little bookshelf. Teela loved it too, and always looked forward to reading time. They were halfway through the book, slowed by Kinsley's constant questions and pointing out of various details in colorful illustrations, when someone tapped on the door.

"Oh! Somebody's heoh, Mommy." Kinsley squirmed to be let down. "Who is it?" she called.

"Kinsley! I've asked you not to do that, sweetheart. Mommy will answer the door. You wait here." She plunked her daughter back on the rocker, hiding a grin at the sudden thundercloud on the little face.

The door did not offer a helpful peephole—not that she felt in the least threatened in Toni's home. "Yes?"

"Teela? I'm not sure you'll remember me, but we met here once before. It's me, Booth Meadows."

What? Not a chance. She shot a glance back at the bed, half expecting to see her sleeping form there, curled up beneath the cozy covers. But she was awake—wide awake.

Booth was here, at Inn the Hollow? Again...at the same time as her? She'd never believed in coincidences, and even if she did, this one was just too unbelievable, *too* coincidental.

"You gonna let the nice man in, Mommy?"

Teela stared at Kinsley. Was this another of her daughter's

"seeing" moments? How could she possibly know Booth was a nice man?

Except that, now and then, Kinsley had a way of knowing things she shouldn't know.

She pulled in a steadying breath and swung the door open. "Booth? I can't believe this. What—what are you doing here?"

"I actually just arrived. Toni mentioned that you were here. She remembered us both having visited in the fall, and sent me up to let you know she's getting ready to sing in the living room. If you haven't heard her, believe me, you won't want to miss this." He grinned. "Wow, I can't believe you're here. Would you...maybe...come on down with me?"

"I'd love to! Thank you, Booth. Let me get Kinsley ready—she's with me this time—and we'll be down in a moment."

She started to shut the door, but a little hand held it open.

"Hi, Mistow Man!"

"Kinsley!" Teela shook her head and shot Booth an apologetic look. "I told her to stay back, but her curiosity is beyond control. Honey, this is Mr. Meadows, not Mr. Man."

Booth grinned and knelt on one knee to look the child in the face. "Hello, young lady. My name is Booth Meadows, but you can call me Booth, if Mommy thinks that's all right. Shall I call you Miss Kinsley?"

She giggled. "Yoah funny. I'm only Kinsley, Mistow Booth."

"Oh, I see, Only Kinsley. I'm only Booth."

She shook her head, and silky hair swung wildly. "I hafta ask Mommy 'bout that, Mistow Booth." She smiled, and two dimples danced into view. "Ah we goin' ta sing?"

He chuckled. "Well, I hope you and your mommy will come downstairs and listen to Toni sing. Trust me, Sweetcake, you don't want me to sing."

Another giggle. Teela swallowed a sigh. Apparently Mr. Booth's charm was every bit as lethal to little girls as to grown-up ones.

Booth stood. "See you ladies downstairs then?"

"We'll be right there, after I lay down a few rules for this talkative little munchkin."

"I'll save seats for you both."

He walked away. Teela closed the door and leaned back against it.

All those months of dreaming and imagining. All that time, thinking she'd never see him again. Yet here he was, right where he first captured her attention.

Why did he have to be so sweet to Kinsley? The charmer! He'd just made himself even more attractive to Teela.

Kinsley wasn't worried about Booth at the moment. "Wules? What kinda wules, Mommy?" She planted a chubby hand on each hip and sighed. "Did I do sometin' bad?"

"No, darling, of course not. You're never bad." Teela swept the child up into her arms. "You just have to be very quiet downstairs because everyone wants to hear Toni sing. You know how upset you get if I talk while you're watching a movie?"

A tiny nose scrunched up. Eyebrows drew downward over green eyes.

"'Cause I can't hear what thayoh saying when you talk, Mommy."

"Exactly. It's hard to hear a song if someone is talking too."

"Okay, Mommy. I won't say nuffin." Kinsley touched a finger to her lips and shook her head. "But can we go now? Huh? I want to heow a song."

Teela chose to let the little one's poor word choice slide…this time. "Come on then, let's get your night clothes on, just in case you fall asleep before I get you back upstairs."

Kinsley frowned. "I just wakeded up!"

"It's been longer than you think, sweetie. And you don't have to go to sleep, but I'd like you to be in your nightclothes anyway, just in case we're down there awhile. Look, I'm in my scuzzies too."

Kinsley rolled her eyes. "Scuzzies isn't the same as sleepin' cloze."

"Well, they can be. I've been known to sleep in sweat things when it's very cold."

"But it's only kinda, a tiny *bit* not wahm today."

"That's true. Still…" She tugged a little sleeper top over Kinsley's head and straightened it around the bottoms she'd slid onto the little one while she tried to make her point. "I'd like you to wear these."

"Can I wayoh my new wobe too?"

"Of course." She held up the little fuzzy pink garment and Kinsley slipped her arms in the sleeves. Teela tied the sash around it. "You look so pretty, darling. Now, let's make your hair all shiny." She lifted the child onto the vanity counter and ran a brush through the tangled strands. When they were smooth, she pulled it all back, deftly created a thick braid, and then clipped a barrette at the end. "There you go. You'll be the belle of the ball."

Like always, her heart did a quick little jig when Kinsley smiled.

"I'm not a bell, Mommy. I'm a gowul."

"Maybe so, but you know what? Mommy's heart rings like a bell…" She touched a finger to Kinsley's nose. "Every time...you…" The finger moved to a tiny dimple on one cheek. "Smile." She slid her wandering finger to her daughter's lips.

Kinsley wrapped her arms around Teela's neck and squeezed. "I love you too, Mommy," she whispered.

Teela closed her eyes and held her daughter close—just

17

long enough to make her squirm. "Well, come on then, Kinny Kat. Let's go hear Miss Toni sing."

Kinsley ran to the door. "Yep. And Mistoh Booth's waitin' foh us. Come on, Mommy, let's go."

Chapter 3

IF SHE WASN'T AN ANGEL, then angels didn't exist.

Booth ordered himself not to stare at Teela, but his eyes refused to accept commands. They strayed her direction often, and lingered long. She mesmerized him, as did the child, Kinsley. Teela called her Kinny Kat a couple of times, and the nickname caught Booth's fancy. The kid looked like a Kinny Kat. Small, wiggly, cuddly. Utterly adorable.

A dozen big, red flags set up a noisy whip-and-flap in his mind...and still he couldn't look away. Couldn't stop wondering what if...

What if Teela Vincent actually gave him a second glance?

She didn't, other than the occasional shy peek and tiny smile—which she bestowed on everyone else in the room as well.

What if he *could* be a dad?

He couldn't. Not a chance.

What if the opportunity arose to hold Teela in his arms?

It wouldn't and he couldn't.

So stop already. Man up and admit she's out of your league, out of your reach, and out of your life.

Booth swallowed a sigh. He'd once wasted a whole year trying out the ultra-modern version of the American dream—the pedigreed dog, the luxury car, the expensive condo on the beach—even the pretend wife, whose aversion to total commitment proved every bit as adamant as his own. That semi-union fell apart when he realized it wasn't real and simply walked out, leaving behind a woman who'd needed a whole week to notice he wasn't there. Good thing they'd both made it clear from the get-go that children wouldn't be a part of their world. She just didn't want to be a mother. Too stressful and messy, and pregnancy might ruin her perfect body. He simply refused to have a child depending on him to be a good father. Or a wife who wanted a dedicated, loving, lifetime husband. He had no idea how to deal with kids, and besides, deadbeat dads ran through his lineage like sap through a maple tree. Disappearing husbands too.

The last few pieces of his ninth birthday cake had still been in the refrigerator when his dad went for a walk and forgot the way home. His paternal grandfather had a second family hidden away in a town fifty miles from Booth's grandmother and their children. When she discovered his secret life, her husband chose his new family and abandoned the old one. Great Granddad Meadows threw in the towel shortly after his young wife delivered their one and only child. The story was that he stopped his tractor in the middle of the field one day, walked into town and caught a ride on a freight train. He simply disappeared, and the family never heard from him after that. Who knew how many other Meadows men before Booth wore the Deadbeat Dad hat?

Growing up, he'd heard all the stories, all the gossip, all the conjecture—and he'd made himself a vow that he'd never be 'that guy.' As an adult, he'd figured out that the only way to make sure he didn't follow in those shameful footsteps was to deny himself the joy of family.

So far, he'd never been in any danger of giving in.

But Teela and her little Kinny Kat might be the end of that boast. Already he felt himself drowning in his self-inflicted banishment from marriage and kids. He couldn't let himself go down that road. Therein lay too much pain and a great deal of heartache for people other than himself.

All of which added up to one thing. He needed to steer clear of Teela Vincent, even though every cell, every molecule, each nerve ending in his body wanted to capture her in his arms and never let go.

She chose that moment—right in the middle of Toni's beautiful Cherokee rendition of Amazing Grace—to look up and straight into Booth's eyes. A smile like pure, gorgeous, radiant sunshine shone into his heart and claimed it forever.

Oh, boy. You're in trouble, dude. Bad, bad trouble.

Yet he couldn't think of a place in the whole world he'd rather be than right where he was, with Teela Vincent sitting close to him on the crowded sofa, and little Kinny Kat snuggled against his chest, quiet and still, wrapped up in the sound of a familiar hymn sung in an unfamiliar tongue.

Oh, yeah. He could be happy to be in this kind of moment for a really long time.

When the gates opened at the nearby wildlife refuge the next morning, Teela and her squirming, barely contained, super-excited little girl were first in line for entry.

Kinsley hit the opening at a run, forcing Teela to trot a little to keep her in sight.

"Kinny Kat! Slow down," she called. "Wait for Mommy. We talked about this, remember?"

The child reluctantly slowed to a stop, then turned to wait. "I 'memboh," she muttered when her mother caught up. "I 'pos'a stay weal close to you all day, 'cause I might get losted." Her eyebrows met in the middle, and she peered up at Teela from beneath them. "Ah you 'fwaid I might get eated up if a big ol' lion sees me all by myself?"

Teela chuckled, even as she took half a moment to catch her breath. She grabbed Kinsley's hand to avoid a repeat performance.

"I'm not afraid of that at all. The nice people who work here keep the animals locked into their areas, all nice and tight, so they can't get out and eat up little Kinny Kats."

Kinsley's answering giggle might well be the sweetest sound this side of Heaven.

"Thayohs only one Kinny Kat, Mommy."

"You've got that right, sweet girl. You're the only you in the whole wide world."

Inside the huge gift shop, they stopped at a counter designated for tour sign-ups. Kinsley was not happy to find they'd have to wait a whole fifteen minutes to get started.

"We'll be out there in no time," Teela assured her. "Be patient, sweetie. Remember your book? What does it say about patience?"

Kinsley sighed, but gave a reluctant nod. "Patience is a vochoo."

Teela bit back a chuckle. "Yes, and what is a virtue?"

"Evwything good in peoples is a vochoo. If we don't have vochoos, we ah *bad* peoples."

Without a hint of amusement, Teela nodded. "Pretty close, munchkin."

She glanced around the room. All manner of animal gifts and goodies graced the shelves. Kinsley should have a stuffed animal or something, but not just yet. She'd wait to see which of the wild animals most fascinated her daughter throughout the day.

A sudden gasp caught in her throat as her gaze skimmed

the ticket counter. Booth stood there, smiling at the clerk as he pulled a wallet from his pocket. Was he here for a tour, as well?

Despite Kinsley's persistent tugs on her hand, she remained fixated on Booth. He wasn't especially tall—about five-nine, maybe an inch more. Still, he was tall enough. Given her less-than-stately five-foot frame, nine or ten more inches made a big difference. Besides, Booth didn't pack an extra pound anywhere, and a lean body went a long way toward visually lengthening a person.

Her treacherous eyes completely disregarded every stern command to look away, so when he turned from the counter in a quick spin, she found herself locked into the magnetic pull of two gorgeous, velvety brown orbs.

Oh, my! Peepers like that presented a definite danger factor to a woman trying hard not to be attracted to a guy.

She inhaled hard, forcing the breath that had been stuck in her throat to cooperate. Then she managed a shaky smile and what she hoped looked like a carefree wave.

That's all it took. Kinsley's sharp little gaze rode that wave all the way across the room.

"Mistoh Booth!" She tore off across the crowded space—twisting, turning and ducking wherever and whenever necessary. Avoiding sharp elbows, heavy feet and older kids dashing around far too fast for an interior space must've been embedded in her DNA. "Mistoh Booth! Lookee heoh! It's yoah sweetcake. I'm wight heoh!"

For a bachelor, Booth reacted well. He lowered himself to a squat and waited. By the time Kinsley emerged from the crowd at full-speed-ahead, his arms were open. She barreled right into them, as if Booth had been a part of her life forever. Entranced, Teela watched him lift her little girl into a quick hug and then prop her firmly on one arm as he strode across the room.

His smile seemed odd…not quite as warm as usual. Not cold. Not unfriendly. Just odd.

"Hey, there. You ladies hanging out in the wild today?"

Teela chuckled. "Why, yes, we are, Mr. Booth. Kinny Kat and I are here to see some lions and tigers and bears."

He raised a pair of thick, dark eyebrows. "Oh, my!"

"Will you come wiff us, Mistoh Booth?"

Teela gasped. "Kinsley! I'm sure Mister Booth has plans with…someone." Her cheeks burned as she turned to meet an amused pair of brown eyes. "I'm so sorry. Kinsley tends to have very little filter."

"She's three, Teela. And besides, I'd love to join the two of you—it'll be a lot more enjoyable than being on my own. If you don't mind, of course."

She couldn't have held back her smile if she'd tried. "Then you're with us, Mister Booth!"

Just like that, Booth's whole purpose in coming to the refuge went right down the proverbial tubes. His perfect plan—devised during a long, sleepless night—lay in tatters. Yet he couldn't claim any real disappointment.

After being with Teela while listening to Toni sing by the fireplace the previous evening, he'd been unable to stop thinking about her. The way her long, blonde hair swung around her shoulders and face like fine silk, and shone with silvery lights when she moved—and she moved with such amazing grace. Huge, translucent blue eyes sparkled and shone as they chatted between songs, or laughed at Kinsley's antics. And that big, open smile…it crinkled her eyes at the corners and lit up her entire face.

All that, and a sweet, giving, caring personality, as well. How could one woman be so incredibly perfect?

Even after they said good night, Booth couldn't get her off his mind. He'd lain in bed, longing for sleep and forgetfulness. But every time he closed his eyes, Teela danced across his mind in vivid color and exquisite detail. He finally got up and dragged himself to the coffee station in one corner of his room. Amongst the bags of flavored tea tucked into a pretty basket near the coffee pot, he found one labeled 'honey chamomile.' Aha! Maybe that would do the trick. Plucking it from the collection, he grinned. Sometimes events did fall in his favor.

He enjoyed the steaming liquid from a large rocking chair nestled close to a big window that overlooked Toni's gardens. In the wee hours of the morning, nothing moved except the tiny lights strung throughout the area. They twinkled and blinked in the darkness like swarms of fireflies. Here in this place, Booth could almost believe that's what they were, even this early in the year. Some shone steadily, while others flickered off and on at various speeds and beats. Somehow it seemed a bit 'wrong' to think of the lack of natural light outside as darkness, when such a glorious display of luminosity pushed the gloom aside.

Much encouraged that he'd managed a few lucid thoughts free of Teela and her adorable kid, Booth rose, rinsed out his cup, and returned to bed with his mind made up. Steering clear of them wasn't what he wanted, but that's what he'd do. Otherwise, unrelenting thoughts of what he couldn't have might drive him downright mindless.

He'd drifted off to sleep planning a day at the wildlife refuge Chef Jonathan had mentioned as a good place to visit. Sounded like a great idea. Just disappear into 'the wild' for a day, and get his mind back on the right path—which included no women, no children. No love, home, or family—not for a man with a bloodline like his.

What weird twist of fate had brought the one person he most needed to avoid to the same place on the same day? Well, two people, since Kinsley and her mother were a package deal. Besides, the kid had too much individual personality to not be counted.

He'd spotted Teela waving from across the gift shop, and experienced the strangest mixture of emotions. Joy wrestled with sorrow for what he couldn't have. Excitement warred with red flags of warning from his innermost being. Longing battled determination to stay emotion-free.

As if it wasn't already too late for that.

"Mistoh Booth?" A tiny hand touched his face as the little voice rose in volume. "Eauth to Mistoh Booth!"

He blinked and found himself staring into a pair of round, curious green eyes—from about an inch away. Kinsley held his face between both tiny hands, and seemed set on getting a close look into the windows of his soul.

"K—Kinsley!" Teela's attempts to hold back laughter couldn't be called entirely successful, but Booth loved the beautiful color in her cheeks from trying so hard.

He gently removed one set of chubby little fingers from his face so he could turn his head.

"Look at Mommy, Sweetcake. She's a laugh about to happen." He sent Teela a mischievous glance, and then fixed a gaze he hoped came across as curious on Kinsley. "I wonder what's so funny?"

"Mommy, what's so—?"

That did it. A lovely flood of hilarity burst from Teela's rose-petal lips. Booth joined in and—after a moment spent assessing the two crazy adults in her company—so did Kinsley.

Teela managed to tone her amusement down to a less vocal level. She was drying moisture from her cheeks when Kinsley piped up with a serious inquiry.

"Mommy?"

"Y—yes, love?"

"What ah we laughin' at?"

Which got Teela going again. Booth chuckled. "I think we're laughing at me, but I'm not really sure. Doesn't matter though...it's fun to laugh, right?"

"Wight!"

"It should be about time for our tour to start. Where's our trolley?" Teela spoke without a single giggle, but her lips maintained an enchanting upward curve.

Booth was fine with that. He couldn't imagine ever getting tired of that smile.

Chapter 4

"YOU'RE RIGHT." BOOTH SET KINSLEY on her feet next to her mother. "I'll go check on it."

As he made his way toward the counter, something caught his eye. Three big, red balloons floated over a small mountain of stuffed animals squeezed onto a long shelf. Above the display, a large red sign bore a message in flowery lettering probably meant to be romantic.

MAKE HER HEART RACE.
GIVE YOUR VALENTINE A WILD THING!

Cheesy, but effective—at least, it was working on him. All the way to the counter and back, his thoughts stayed busy. Crazy busy. Santa Monica Freeway busy.

Hadn't the New Year just started a week or so ago? A quick peek into his mental calendar told him today was the tenth of February. Only four days until the annual day of romance. How had he lost so much time?

And why was he even concerned about it? He didn't have a Valentine, wild or otherwise.

Still, by the time he returned to where Teela waited with an ever-more-impatient youngster, a plan was taking shape in his mind. She might not be *his* Valentine, but she deserved to feel special to someone on Valentine's Day. Kinsley too.

He didn't have a lot more time to dwell on it. He'd no

sooner told Teela that the tour trolley was on the way than the vehicle appeared outside the big, open "barn doors."

"Yay!" Kinsley yelled.

She squirmed, but Teela refused to let go of her hand. Booth watched the silent struggle, amused. Finally he lifted Kinsley up onto one arm, grabbed Teela's hand and strode toward the open trolley.

The smiling tour guide behind the wheel jumped out to help settle them inside.

"Howdy, folks!" The man's deep, rumbling voice came as a startling contrast to his rather scrawny frame. "I'm Mike, and I'll be tellin' y'all about the animals we see on our tour." He gave Teela a polite nod. "Any time you want these wheels to stop rollin, y'all just speak up and say so, hear? Little Miss might need to stretch her legs now and then—or you might. Don't matter the reason. You want to stop, we stop. I am at your service, and there's no set timeframe for us to be back here."

"Thank you." Teela shone a radiant smile on the man.

Booth bit back a grin. *Poor guy won't be able to tell lion from tiger from bear after that.*

But Mike proved stronger than he looked. From the first turn of the wheels, they were thrust into an unforgettable day of tour-guide humor, interesting facts about individual animals—some fun, some sad, some downright horrifying—and amazing close-up views of wild creatures many people never got to see, even at a distance.

Information about the animals taken in by the wildlife refuge after being in sadly abusive situations clearly touched Teela's compassionate heart. Her eyes misted, and this time they weren't happy tears. Booth got it, completely. Some of the tales even had him clearing his throat a little, even though the guide obviously left out the more graphic details in deference to "Little Miss."

Kinsley took particular notice of the lions. Several of the magnificent beasts wandered the property. They cast a glance toward the trolley, even eyed the humans as they stood outside the fences now and then, but seemed mostly unaffected. Clearly, human traffic around the refuge had long since become of little interest to the animals.

At one stop, they were all amazed when one of the lions drew close and stood just on the other side of the fence. After a moment, he rubbed his huge, black-maned head against the barrier. Mike knelt to place a hand against the fence, stroking the animal the best he could. Soft, comforting words spilled from his lips.

"Hey, Shivar. You're lookin' mighty fine today...like a genuine King of the Jungle." He shook his head. "Though I don't know where that term came from, since lions live on the savannah...the grasslands...not the forests—at least, not as a rule. But you look quite regal, no matter where you live." He continued to stroke the animal's fur. "Did you know these folks come all the way out here just to visit you, Lion King Shivar? That's what you are, you know, even though you've been dragged from your natural home and put in this cage. I'm sorry 'bout that, but it's the only way we know to take care of you, since you can't go back home." He looked up and caught Kinsley staring at the huge animal. "You know, I think Little Miss might like to say howdy too. Much as you like attention, you'll be just fine with that, won't you?"

He smiled at Kinsley, and then slid his gaze to Teela. "That all right with you, ma'am?"

"Of course!" Teela knelt beside her daughter. "Would you like to pet Shivar, Kinny Kat?"

The little one shook her head...nodded...shook her head...and then gave a firm, definitive dip of a tiny chin. "Will you stand wight by me, Mommy?"

"Always, baby girl. Come on, let's talk to King Shivar."

Booth caught his breath. They were safe. He knew that. So why did his stomach suddenly tighten up like a wet knot in a fisherman's rope?

Lord, is this what it's like to be a dad? A husband?

Good thing he'd written off being a family man. He wasn't at all sure even his physical heart could handle it.

Teela led Kinsley close to Mike. Kinsley's hand put up a bit of a struggle, and Teela forced herself not to hold so tight.

Shivar stretched out on the ground and pressed his side flush against the fence, eager for the attention he loved—just like any cat. Mike took Kinsley's little hand and ran it over the lion's fur, which pushed through the diamond pattern in the fencing.

"Oh!" The child's eyes widened. "It's not veowy soft."

"You're right, it's not." Mike shook his head. "It's coarse, and it helps protect him against weather and against other animals that might attack. He's very soft on his belly though."

"My kitty is soft. Mommy said lions ah just gweat big kitty cats."

Mike chuckled. "Well, in some ways, they are. They love to play with toys and with each other. Shivar has a big ball that he bounces around sometimes." He stopped to grin at Booth and Teela when Kinsley burst into sweet giggles, no doubt imagining the huge cat playing like a house kitten. "They don't climb a lot, but they're very curious." The guide stood, his lighthearted expression dimming a bit. "They're also dangerous, Little Miss. They're big and strong and meat is

32

what they like to eat. So if they're hungry, it's not a good idea to be around them."

"They eat *peoples*?" Kinsley's eyes grew round.

"Sometimes, yes…I'm afraid they do." Mike stroked a hand against the not-so-soft fur that made its way through the fence. Then he grinned, clearly glad to think of a better subject. "Did you know these big guys can sing?"

Kinsley giggled. When Mike just raised his eyebrows and sent her a wry grin, she bit at her bottom lip, clearly uncertain. Finally she turned to Teela. "Mommy?"

"Well, I haven't had an opportunity to hear them, sweetheart, but I've read that they really do sing when the sun goes down, and also in the very early morning. It's called caroling, like at Christmas time." She looked at Mike. "Is that right?"

"Right as rain." The man indicated the trolley, and they all climbed back in. "Stick around a few hours and maybe you can sing with them. There'll be a whole pride of lions joining in the chorus."

"I would so love to do that." Teela smiled, her mind filled with ideas most people might consider a little odd. Not only singing with the lions…but might she be able to dance to their song? "It must be a powerful tune."

"That it is. A powerful tune indeed."

The remainder of the tour was quieter than the first part. Kinsley snuggled up in Booth's arms, her eyes barely open. She'd missed her nap time, and the struggle was real.

Teela couldn't imagine sleeping in Booth's arms, with her head resting on his chest. She'd be wide awake, every individual nerve on edge, each of her senses so highly tuned that sleep would a "non-thing"…maybe forever.

She lifted her gaze from her sleepy child and found Booth watching her. He shot her that mind-numbing crooked smile and her face warmed…but she didn't look away. She couldn't. Her fingers itched to touch the barely there cleft in his chin—a strong chin, but far from protruding. Just well-defined, like his jawline. Her gaze traveled that line and landed on his lips.

Her breath caught in her throat. *Lord, what am I thinking? My mind is going places I can't let it go. Help me be strong!*

She released a silent sigh.

Strong? Right now, she couldn't even remember what the word meant. Not with Booth cuddling Kinsley like she was the most precious thing on earth. Not when he smiled like he was right now…one side of his lips taking a short trip upward in that adorable, heart-stopping, lop-sided grin. And certainly not with those velvety-soft eyes drinking her in like she was a refreshing spring in the desert.

It didn't help that she was kinda-sorta-almost certain the same kind of thoughts were bouncing around in his head at this moment—like distant dance partners for her own wayward imaginings. And wayward they absolutely were. Because this…whatever *this* was between Booth and her…couldn't go anywhere. Certainly not now, and probably not ever.

First and foremost…Kinsley. That little girl in Booth's arms held so much of Teela's heart. How could she possibly find enough love for someone else? Aside from that, her job as a dance instructor took up more hours of her life than she liked, even though she loved teaching dance. And yet another reason—she spent countless hours of her "free" time practicing with the praise dance team. The other members had slowly but surely edged her into the role of "team leader," though it wasn't a position she'd set out to obtain. She danced with the team because she loved to worship God through every avenue available—and dance was her God-given, creative gift. Why shouldn't she use it for Him?

With all that going on, she had no time—*no* time!—for

men. She was busy. Way, way too busy.

"Hey, Teela?"

"Mmm?" Despite her busy brain, drowsiness was beckoning her as well.

"Would you come back here with me on Friday night?"

She opened her mouth, but Booth held up a finger.

"It'll be an overnight thing. I'll reserve a couple of cabins—one for you and Sweetcake. The other for me." He gave her that grin—the one that ought to be illegal. "The cabins come with tickets to a concert unlike any you've ever attended. Will you come back with me to hear the lions sing?"

She had stopped breathing about the time Booth said, "Hey, Teela." The little naysayers in her brain set up a quick-step of reasons not to accept. Valid reasons. Inarguably *good* reasons, like the ones she'd already gone over and over…and over.

Her breath whooshed out and her lips formed a great big smile—a smile for which she had not given the go-ahead. "Oh, Booth…I would *love* that! Of course I'll come."

Chapter 5

TEELA EASED OUT OF BED and into the bathroom. She'd set her alarm to rise early and get in some time with her Father before the whole world woke up. The gardens behind Inn the Hollow seemed a perfect place for prayer.

She'd missed her early morning chats with God since she and Kinsley left Sugar Land. Not that she hadn't prayed. The line was open between her and the Lord twenty-four-seven, and she often sent up quick prayers—thanked Him for the beauty around her, sent up a plea for wisdom and patience when dealing with Kinsley, or simply said, "I love you, Father." She'd done that a lot since they'd been on vacation, especially here at Inn the Hollow. Everywhere she looked, her gaze fell on new reminders of how perfectly He'd created the world for His children. When that happened, she always took a moment to let Him know she noticed.

But she longed for serious prayer time. A time of genuine communion with her Father.

After that unforgettable day at the refuge, she needed quality time with her Creator, the Lover of her soul. Only He could give her the strength she needed to resist her growing feelings for Booth—whom she hadn't seen at all in the past two days. Was he backing off? But they had a "date" tomorrow night…didn't they? Was he regretting having asked her to return to the refuge with him?

She ignored the tightness in her chest at that thought. Maybe he would regret it so much that he'd bow out—gracefully, of course. He was such a gentleman. But still, it would eliminate her concern about spending too much time with him, growing too close. Becoming emotionally attached.

Yes, she needed prayer time. Not just a casual prayer-thought, but deep spirit-prayer.

So she slipped out of the room after touching her lips to Kinsley's soft cheek. The little one rarely awakened before 7:30 a.m., sometimes even later. Teela would be back before that.

Still, she stuck her head into the kitchen before heading outside. As she had hoped, Carla was there and already busy breaking eggs into a huge bowl. She looked up when Teela took a hesitant step into the room.

"Teela! Good morning, dear." She smiled, one eyebrow hiked playfully upward. "I can tell you need something. What is it? If it's in this kitchen, it's yours."

Teela laughed softly. "Well, it is in this kitchen, Carla. It's you. I'd like to spend a little while in the garden before everyone else wakes up. Would you mind looking in on Kinsley once or twice? She's sleeping soundly, and I don't expect her to move a muscle before I'm back inside, but just in case…? I don't want her to awaken and be frightened."

"I don't mind in the least, Miss Teela. I'll keep an eye on the little one. You go on outside, and enjoy your prayer time."

How does Carla know I'm going out to pray? I don't think I told her why I'm going to the garden.

No matter. She trusted the woman, and Kinsley seemed quite taken with her. With Carla watching out for her daughter, Teela could pray without being half focused on the suite upstairs.

In the garden, she breathed in the sweet, clean smell of the hollow. Pine, magnolia and hickory trees in the wooded area behind the inn combined with various winter blooms in Toni's garden to create a strong, sweet aroma—pansies, violas, camellias. Others too, most of them unfamiliar. Teela closed her eyes, lifted her face to the sky and smiled. She could talk to the Lord anywhere, but this…this was like doing so in a little corner of Heaven.

She drifted further into the hedges and shrubs laid out in neat sections, loving the way the skirt of her praise-dancing garment flowed against her legs. On a whim, while dressing to come outside, she'd slipped it on, laughing at herself a little for even bringing the rather elaborate dress along, but for whatever reason, she'd been unwilling to leave it behind. She might as well wear it while praying at Inn the Hollow. No other need for it would arise until she returned home.

As she moved further in, closer to the woods, praise bubbled up from deep inside. Hummingbirds darted about, seemingly undaunted by the human in their midst. Every few moments, a butterfly fluttered by. Had they been aroused from their quiescent rest by the hummingbirds…or perhaps by Teela herself? She tried to move quietly and gracefully, but she'd never be able to match the grace of these beautiful creatures of nature.

Father, thank You for this beautiful morning, and these glorious beings here to pray with me.

She swayed a little—an unplanned preparatory move to take her deeper into prayer mode. Just before she would have closed her eyes, motion off to one side caught her attention. Despite knowing there'd been a bear incident in the woods behind this very inn only months earlier, she wasn't frightened. No place for fear or stress existed in this peaceful garden. Turning her head, she pulled in a surprised breath.

Toni stood in the next section of hedges, eyes closed, face

lifted toward the sky. Hummingbirds lined both outstretched arms. A few of the tiny creatures perched on her shoulders, and others nestled into the palms of both cupped hands.

Fascinated, Teela stood statue-still. She noted the movement of Toni's lips, and somehow knew her hostess was in the garden to pray, just as she was. The Native American woman *shone* in the early morning light. Long, straight black hair flowed over her shoulders and down her back, its sheen almost too bright to be real.

Halo?

Teela pulled in another deep breath. Where in the world had that come from?

Toni's body dipped low, and both arms lifted high, her hands bent in a perfect ballerina's *port de bras*. Then, slowly and with unbelievable grace, she stood tall, but lowered her arms—just to a straight-out position, clearly unwilling to frighten the tiny creatures perched along their length. Again and again, she repeated the dip-and-sway of her prayer dance. Soft words spilled from her lips. Teela couldn't hear them, but she suspected many of them were spoken in the native tongue of the dancer's ancestors.

Then Toni began to sing—and no doubt remained. She sang a Cherokee praise song.

Teela found herself dancing along. Tears welled in her eyes and she let them fall as she swayed and spun in an unrehearsed, completely spontaneous series of movements, even as she poured her heart out to God in sincere worship. Never had she experienced such an overwhelming degree of close communication and conversation with her Maker. No congregation watched. No one but God listened.

So she praised. She worshipped. Eyes closed, hands raised, Teela danced with total abandon. She danced only for God. And He danced with her.

Booth left his room, careful to make as little noise as possible. Other guests slept behind the closed doors on each side of the upstairs hall. Rousing them from their enviable slumber wasn't in his plan.

He hadn't found that enviable state for more than a few hours since he spent the day with Teela and Kinsley at the wildlife refuge. Couldn't get his mind off the two of them…especially Teela. But then, what did he expect? He hadn't stopped thinking about her since they first met, right here at this bed and breakfast, six months ago. Like him, she'd been here only for a really short time. They'd had a single chat, and Teela shared more than he'd hoped for when he asked to join her at her table in the dining room. But the next morning, she was gone as if she'd never been there at all, leaving Booth to half-wonder if he'd completely lost his mind.

His return to Hummingbird Hollow had come about solely because of Teela. Some weeks ago, he'd arrived at a possible solution to his mental madness.

He had to return to the place he met her. She wouldn't be there, and maybe that's what he needed—a mental picture of Inn the Hollow that did not include Teela Vincent. After mulling it over for another couple of weeks that seemed overly long, he made arrangements for a colleague to handle his appointments for a couple of weeks, and then headed to Arkansas.

His flight was behind, and then he had to wait for a rental car. Those setbacks threw his schedule off, putting him at Inn the Hollow after dinner time. Jonathan Savage—incredible chef and lifelong friend to the lodge owner, Toni Littlebird— insisted on bringing out a plate for Booth when he arrived.

Toni stopped by while he ate.

"I'm so glad you found your way back to our little hollow. Your last visit was way too short." She hesitated. "I hope you won't think this is strange, but I really felt your Hollow experience wasn't complete when you left in August. There's something more for you here, Booth Meadows."

Booth eyed the beautiful Native American woman. Toni was amazing, and a talented singer, but...really? What was she even talking about?

She laughed softly. "I know, it sounds strange, but trust what I say. The Father has given me a gift that a lot of people cannot accept. I hope you can, because I speak the truth. Daddy God has something special for you in this place. Don't leave without it, okay?"

Booth swallowed the last bite of Chef Savage's delicious spinach-stuffed chicken breast served with moist, flavorful rice pilaf and sweet peas. He kept his gaze on his hostess's face. Nothing but the utmost sincerity could be found there.

"I will keep an open mind."

Toni smiled. "That's all I ask. Now, if you'll excuse me, I have to get my guitar. Come on into the big room, if you'd like. I'll be singing a few songs in half an hour or so."

She waved and started out of the room, and then turned. "Oh, would you do me a favor, please? I didn't tell anyone I'd be singing tonight. I hadn't really planned on it, but Daddy God is nudging me in that direction." She smiled, and Booth's heart melted. He suspected God's gift to Toni was, in fact, that magic, irresistible smile. "Would you mind going upstairs and letting one of my other guests know? She was down for dinner a short time ago, so she won't have gone to bed already. Would you be a dear and just knock on the door of room two? Tell her I asked you to invite her down. Her name is Teela Vincent."

Booth nearly choked on a drink of sweet tea.

Toni blinked, and then her eyes widened. "Oh, that's right! You and Teela were here at the same time last fall, weren't you...just briefly?"

"Yes, I met her then. We were both here the day Cass and Ryder spent some time hiding from a very angry mother bear in a cave not far from your little chapel."

"Yes! I remember now. Teela left the next morning, so you couldn't have known her well, but I recall seeing the two of you chatting after dinner that night. Well, that's perfect. You won't feel so awkward about inviting her down." She spun and headed for the door. "Sorry to dash off like this, but I have to get that guitar. Thanks for helping me out with this, Booth!"

Then she was gone. Booth drew a sigh and blew it out slowly.

Teela. Right here at the same bed and breakfast where they'd originally met. Again. So much for being able to visualize the inn without her in it.

He wasn't much of a believer in coincidence. So what was this all about? Could there be something to Toni's goings-on about God having something for him here? Could it possibly be Teela...because, if so, the lodge owner's "Daddy God" must be having a senior moment. He, more than anyone, knew that Booth couldn't have Teela.

He couldn't have a serious relationship with anyone—and marriage? Well, that was certainly out of the picture.

Still, he'd promised Toni he'd let Teela know she was singing. That much he could do.

The memory brought a sigh as he reached the door leading out onto the gardens. Maybe he should've turned around that night, and walked out the front door instead of going upstairs to get Teela. Because now his heart was all tangled up in her and Kinsley, and he had to find a way to break that connection.

He should have headed back to Hollywood—back to his job counseling the rich and famous. He snorted. The majority of his clientele didn't need him, but having a therapist was 'in.' Booth supposed that ridiculous mindset meant job security, in his case. But he'd been counseling folks who didn't need it for a mighty long time—and in doing so, he'd lost all the satisfaction and fulfillment his chosen career should have provided. He'd wanted to help people—real people, with real issues. Instead, he'd become a high-society icon, helping the pampered privileged try to fill an inner emptiness with riches and power. He's sickened now by the knowledge that he has encouraged them in that quest, when he knows it won't work. It certainly hasn't for him.

Outside, the air proved only cool enough to be pleasant against his skin. Unless Old Man Winter had a change of heart and made an abrupt turnaround, Lady Spring would move in a bit early this time around. Booth didn't object. He much preferred soothing sunshine to biting cold.

He'd grabbed a mug of coffee on his way through the dining room, and carried it with him now as he moved into the neat hedge rows. Oh, what an awesome aroma! California had a lot going for it, but clean, great-smelling air wasn't among its best qualities.

A hummingbird darted close and hovered not two feet in front of Booth's face.

"Whoa!" The exclamation burst from his lips in a whispered shout, if such a thing existed. Something about this garden inspired peacefulness, not noise.

He stopped mid-step, unwilling to send the tiny creature flitting away.

"Well, good morning, little guy." What would his big-shot clients think of their therapist if they could see him now…whispering to a bird? But he didn't dare speak any louder—he might scare the tiny creature away. "What're you up to this morning—besides blocking my path?"

The hummer remained where he was, close enough for Booth to see the separate strands in his bright blue feathers. Then he darted off.

Booth smiled a little. "I guess that's permission to enter his territory."

He'd taken only two steps before the bird zoomed back in and brought him to a stop again.

"Miss me already, little dude?"

The hummingbird zoomed away, but only a few feet. Then he hovered, as if…waiting?

Booth narrowed his gaze. Was it possible the hummer wanted him to follow? Toni said God had something for him here. Maybe his tiny friend wanted to reveal that gift.

"All right then." He dashed what remained of his coffee beneath a hedge, hooked the handle on one finger and spoke to the little bird who apparently wanted to be a trail guide. "Lead on, little one."

As if he understood Booth's words, the hummer took off. He didn't zoom across the hedges, but flew in a straight line with the paths.

So Booth could follow…?

Okay, "Daddy God." I'll play along. He followed the tiny bird down the first path and onto another. As he rounded the curve onto the third row, something moved in his peripheral vision. He swung around to see what was there, and caught his breath in a painful gasp.

Across a couple of hedged-enclosed spaces, Teela danced. She moved with all the grace Booth remembered from watching her on *Save a Dance for Me*, the competition television show on which he'd first seen her. The brand new light of morning lent a crimson glow to the flowing, rose-colored garment that floated around her.

Even without the white robe, she's angelic.

He caught his breath at the thought, because in that instant, he knew. Teela wasn't out in the garden in the early morning, swaying around to get in a little exercise. This dance was an offering of praise. Her gorgeous face was raised heavenward, hands lifted in the same direction, waving back and forth in perfect synchrony with her body.

Even as he stood in utter awe, watching the lovely woman praise God with her entire being, another dancer came into view.

Several benches were interspersed throughout the garden area. Booth dropped onto the nearest one, both hands raised to cover his lips. Just beyond the square of hedges in which Teela worshipped, Toni swayed and dipped in a dance style all her own. Hummingbirds lined her arms, perched on her shoulders, nestled into her hands. She lifted her arms high, lowered them as she stood tall and straight—possibly on her tiptoes, though Booth couldn't see her feet to verify that assumption. Over and again, she made similar motions, and not once did a hummingbird startle away. Like Teela, she lifted her face heavenward. Her lips moved, and though he couldn't hear her words, he knew.

Toni was praying. So was Teela. Yet neither of them seemed aware of the other.

Booth found himself unable to look away. The women's prayer time, their dances, their sincere worship…he'd never witnessed anything so glorious…never experienced anything so powerful. On its own, Teela's praise dance stirred his soul. Combined with Toni's hummingbird prayer-dance, it was almost too much to take in.

How long had it been since he'd prayed—really prayed, with his whole heart, soul, body and mind focused on being with the Father? How long since he'd felt anything remotely close to the Spirit-waves that rocked his entire being in this moment?

He blinked back sudden moisture that burned his eyes, and then gave up and let the tears fall as he bowed his head and joined the women in prayer.

Chapter 6

BOOTH DIDN'T STAY LONG. HE wanted to be gone before either Toni or Teela knew he'd witnessed their morning meditations.

Not that he'd planned that unexpected peek into their morning prayers. He'd been led there. That tiny blue-feathered creature had taken him right where he needed to be for the best view in the garden. No bird does something like that without a Higher Power being in control. Booth no longer doubted that God had directed his steps back to this place, just as the lodge hostess had told him. Still, he needed some quiet time for prayer and introspection before he spoke with Teela, and definitely before he could tell her that he'd witnessed her prayer dance.

He might never find words to express how that dance had affected him, what a powerful experience it was, but if the moment came when it felt right to do so, he would try.

Back in his room, he stretched out on the bed, closed his eyes and brought his mind into focus. Right now, he just wanted to think about his life, what was wrong with it and what was right. Meditating on the Lord would help him get things mentally aligned for improvement.

But God had other plans.

After struggling for days to find rest, a heaviness took hold of his eyelids, right along with the mind-drift that always preceded genuine sleep. Then something else happened—a letting-go within his soul. A release of things to which he'd held so tightly for far too long. A surrender of self and a taking-in of Christ.

A breath burst from his lips like a physical departure of the old Booth, creating a brand new space for the new man…a Booth in step with his Creator. He drew in another deep breath, and pulled it deeper still. *Come in, Father. Be present within me every day, every hour, every moment that I live.*

A satisfied smile tugged at his lips. He allowed them to curve upward, since God seemed to want that smile. And then sleep claimed him.

Teela enjoyed a quiet breakfast in the dining room the next morning, after another peaceful prayer time. Few guests were up and about at this hour. One man entered the room long enough to pile a plate with toast and a handful of jelly packets, and fill a mug with coffee. He placed both on a tray, gave Teela a polite nod, and headed back upstairs.

She finished her own toast and boiled egg, then sat at the table for a short time. Outside the window, hummingbirds darted in and out of the patio area, visiting the various feeders strewn about the space. Teela smiled, remembering the incredible performance the little creatures had put on during her brief stop here in the fall.

When she'd met Booth for the first time.

The fact that they both wound up at Hummingbird Hollow twice, at the same time, with no planning on their part seemed a little beyond coincidental. Did God have a hand in it—and if He did, why? His plan couldn't be anything romantic. He knew her heart better than anyone. He knew that marriage was not in the picture—not anytime soon, and possibly never, depending on Kinsley's circumstances as the years passed. Her daughter would be her primary focus as long as she needed Teela in any way. That didn't leave a lot of room for romance, and certainly not for a husband.

She hushed the little voice in her head that suggested Kinsley might need more. A circle that included a mommy and a daddy. A family.

Out of the question. But when she was with Booth, she longed for something more. When he gave her that lopsided smile…when he touched her hand…or when he simply looked at her in that certain way—as if he'd be happy to do nothing but look at her for the rest of his life. In those moments, a longing rose up inside her. Was having both truly beyond hope? Other women had children and a husband. The world was built on families. Why couldn't she have that same blessing?

She sighed. Because she wasn't a real mother. She hadn't carried Kinsley for nine months, and then brought her into the world through the pain of childbirth. That she absolutely adored the child she now considered her own did not make her a mother in the true sense of the word. She was a substitute. Because of that, didn't it make sense that she'd have to work twice as hard to be an acceptable mommy to that little girl? Didn't something almost magical happen to women when they actually bore a child…some invisible sprinkling of "mommy dust" that gave them a natural instinct, a secret knowledge about mothering?

Teela believed that to be true, at least to the extent that "real" mothers were born along with the birth of their babies.

That's why her central focus in life was on mothering her friend's motherless child. She would allow nothing—absolutely nothing, including love, to take her focus off Kinsley. When she promised Annalise to take her child in the event of her death, she'd relinquished any right to love, romance, and all the distractions inherent in those things.

She didn't mind the sacrifice. Her love for Kinsley, and Kinsley's love for her…that would be enough.

It had to be enough.

Yet she found herself concerned that Booth hadn't made an appearance the past couple of days. Was he avoiding her? He had to be. How else could two people, moving about the same, moderately-sized bed and breakfast and the grounds surrounding it, not see each other even once in a two-day period? Possible, of course, but not likely.

Well, they'd either be returning to the refuge tonight or they wouldn't. Maybe this would be the answer she needed about her feelings. She knew so little about Booth, yet she'd never before experienced such an all-consuming, magnetic draw to another person.

On second thought, maybe she'd cancel tonight's plans herself, and avoid any possible hurt in the future.

"What's on your mind, Teela?" Toni slid into the other chair at the small table Teela occupied. In a surprise move, she took Teela's hand and held it between both of hers. "I sense a heaviness in your heart."

"Oh!" For half an instant, every instinct urged Teela to recapture her hand, walk away—anything but confide in someone. But this was Toni Littlebird, and something about the woman made that kind of response impossible. In Hummingbird Hollow, in this woman's ancestral home, things simply worked differently…including the habits of a lifetime. "I don't—" She sighed. "I'm so confused."

"Hmm. I don't suppose this confusion has anything at all to do with a certain handsome man from California?"

Teela's gaze flew to meet Toni's. "H–how did you...?" She groaned. "Am I that obvious?"

"No, of course not. Daddy God gave me a little hint." She smiled, patted Teela's hands, and then released them. "Want to talk about it?"

"No, but thank you." Teela grabbed her napkin and started folding it in tiny pleats. After half a moment or so, words began to spill from her lips, despite her determination not to talk. "I can't get involved with anyone, Toni. I've got a little girl to consider."

Low laughter drew her gaze upward, off the napkin in her hand. "And having a child means you can't have romantic love in your life? Teela, look around you, honey. The world is full of women with both husbands and children."

"I know. But what if I can't be both? What if I don't have it in me? My first concern has to be Kinsley...always."

"I get that, but I don't think Kinsley—or her mother— would want you to sacrifice happiness by making her the center of your world."

She shook her head. "Probably not, but I promised Annalise I'd love her child like my own—and I do. I can't risk changing that."

"I see." Toni nodded. "I suppose when you took Kinsley into your heart, you stopped loving your parents as much. After all, God only allots each of us love enough for one person...right?"

Teela's gaze flew to meet the other woman's, only to find Toni's lips curved into a beautiful smile.

She relaxed a bit and managed to relax a little—just enough to return a shadow of her normal smile. "All right, I hear you. But what if—" She broke off and looked out the window, where hummingbirds still flitted back and forth, to and from the patio feeders.

"Teela?"

"Hmmm?" She couldn't quite bring herself to look at her hostess just yet.

"I think you're really more concerned that you might choose a man who won't love Kinsley, or will hurt her in some way."

Teela went still. How did Toni do that? She was right. Teela didn't doubt for an instant her own ability to love Kinsley and keep her safe from harm, but she couldn't foresee another person's behavior. What if she brought a man into their lives who loved her, as a woman, but couldn't love Kinsley?

She couldn't risk that any more than she could risk her own inability to handle a complete family.

Toni's soft words broke through her mini-reverie. "Booth Meadows would harm *himself* before he'd ever hurt you or Kinsley."

She forced her gaze from the antics of the little creatures on the patio to study the other woman's calm, assured expression. "You can't know that."

"And yet I do. So do you, Teela. Look deep into your heart. You'll see." She rose, brushed her fingers lightly over Teela's shoulder, and left the room.

Teela sat a bit longer, soaking in the peace that permeated this old home…digesting the things she'd discussed with her hostess. Pondering Toni's words. *Booth Meadows would harm himself before he'd ever hurt you or Kinsley.*

Why did they ring so true within her soul, now that they had been spoken aloud?

She walked to the window and watched the hummingbirds for a few moments, then turned to head upstairs.

"Good morning, Teela!" Booth wandered in just as she swung away from the window. "All set for the concert tonight?"

So they were still on.

She toned down a smile that wanted to be radiant. Good heavens, she was glad to see him! Too glad, and it frightened her all the way to the tips of her toes.

"I guess so, although I have to admit I was beginning to wonder if you'd changed your mind. You haven't been around at all."

"I had some personal things that had to be dealt with. Spent the last couple of days mostly in my room. I did come down a time or two to talk Jonathan out of a snack, but I didn't see you." He grinned. "That said, we are definitely on for tonight." He glanced around the dining room. "Are you coming or going?"

"I'm headed back up. Kinsley should be awake within about half an hour, give or take a few minutes either way. Her sleeping pattern is pretty predictable, but I'd hate for her to be alone when she wakes up, so…" She glanced more regretfully than she liked at the staircase. "I'd better get going."

"Okay." Booth placed a hand on her shoulder as she turned to go, swinging her back toward him. He touched the fingers of his other hand to her face and trailed them down her jawline, leaving behind a delicious, burning tingle that traveled throughout her entire frame, like a burst of low-watt electricity—not painful, just breathtaking. "I'm looking forward to tonight."

She caught her breath, and dipped her chin. "Me too," she whispered.

Then she whirled and forced herself not to run to the stairs. All the way up, she felt his gaze on her…or she imagined it. Why would he stare at her for that long?

At the top, she risked a backward glance. Sure enough, Booth stood right where she'd left him, his velvet brown gaze fixed on her. His lips lifted in that heart-stopping crooked smile. Then he touched a finger to his lips and swung it back toward her, like an air kiss.

The way Teela's heart danced, he may as well have pulled her into his arms and kissed her plumb silly. Her tummy tightened at the thought.

She whirled and fled to her room.

Chapter 7

SMOOTH AS THE FINEST SATIN, just as he'd imagined it. Booth allowed his fingers to travel Teela's face only for a moment, despite his longing to lose himself in that silky paradise. A strange, prickling heat enveloped the tips of his fingers, even after that all-too-brief touch.

Dear Lord, she's beautiful!

His clenched stomach muscles didn't promise great results if he tried to eat right away. He'd take a walk—or, on second thought, maybe he'd just sit out on the patio for a few minutes and soak in the sunshine…and the positivity. Something about Inn the Hollow made him want to believe everything could, and would, be all right. That he wasn't crazy to be thinking about Teela as far more than just a pretty face.

Maybe, despite all the years of thinking otherwise, he *could* be a husband and father. A family man who would never, ever walk away.

Low laughter rumbled from his lips as he took a seat on a patio bench. *Who are you, man? This isn't the way you think. Ever.*

"What's funny, dude?" Chef Savage stepped through the double glass doors and lowered himself onto a nearby chair. "I could use a chuckle or two myself."

"Hey, Jonathan." Booth smiled. Not only was the big,

Native American man an amazing chef, he was a downright good guy. They had enjoyed a couple of conversations. If they lived close enough to make it a possibility, something told him they'd be friends. "I doubt my thoughts would make anyone chuckle."

"Try me."

"Well, to be honest, I was thinking this place is a little bit magical."

Jonathan laughed. "Magic? I hear what you're saying, but Toni has taught me not to like that word too much."

"I get that. So…not magic, per se. But this place, Jonathan… It isn't just any bed and breakfast. In fact, I think the whole hollow must be bubble-wrapped in something that keeps it protected from the world's negativity. Something that filters out bad thoughts and…oh, I don't know." He shook his head, wishing he'd never let Jonathan draw him into this conversation. "You must think I've lost my mind."

"Not at all." The big man looked off into the garden, his expression unreadable. "You're not the first person to suggest such a thing. There is something special about this hollow. I can't say what it is, because I don't know, but I'll tell you what I think, if you care to hear it."

"Please…" Booth leaned forward, eager for some kind of explanation.

"Well, for starters, this house is so old, Booth. Toni's ancestors who lived within these walls were raised to understand not only American customs and manners, but also the ancient way of the Cherokee. I don't know how you feel about that, but I have a deep respect for them. A lot of wisdom can be found in their teachings."

Booth shrugged. "I have to confess, I'm not familiar enough to say either way."

Jonathan nodded absently. "Not a lot of people are, unless

our blood runs in their veins. Actually, many people who do have Native American ancestry still don't know much about it."

"But you do."

"I do. My family, like Toni's, held to many of the old ways, while being open to new things. My father always says he loves the Cherokee teachings because—despite the wars and massacres and all the violence that ensued during the making of this country—our people come from a place of peace. We know how to separate ourselves from negativity and ugliness of spirit and dwell on a better plane, even if we can only do so on a mental level." He paused and raised his gaze to Booth's, held it, probed it. Booth said nothing, but he must have passed Jonathan's silent test, because the other man nodded and continued.

"I think Hummingbird Hollow, where Toni's ancestors walked, exists on that plane. Not that it isn't part of this world, because…well, of course it is. But a tremendous amount of history exists within these walls—and even on the grounds outside. Add to that Toni's deep faith in 'Daddy God,' her strong devotion to Christ, the prayers that she pours out to Him in these gardens, and…well, this place is literally saturated in a spiritual power that touches every single visitor."

Booth nodded. A week ago, he'd have laughed at such thoughts. Today, he leaned more toward thinking they were far more than the ramblings of a man whose thinking still leaned toward his Native American ancestry. Jonathan spoke truth—at least, insofar as he understood it.

"You said something about having lost your mind? Maybe they'll put us in side-by-side cells." Jonathan's rumbling laughter flowed across the patio and into the gardens like soothing thunder—and Booth didn't think of that phrase as an oxymoron, not in this moment.

He managed a half grin, but he shook his head. "I've changed my mind. We're not crazy. We're just existing on a different plane."

Jonathan nodded. "Good for you. So have you given any thought to our conversation yesterday?"

Booth had surprised himself by opening up to the chef about things he'd never shared—not with anyone. His friend Cass knew him well, but even with her, he kept some things buried in his heart and mind. But this gentle man, whom he barely knew, somehow drew him out, with no pressing, prodding or nudging whatsoever.

"You are still taking Miss Teela and her little one to the 'concert' you mentioned, aren't you?" Jonathan persisted.

"I've thought about little else." The interchange between them had been brief, but intense—like this one. "Thanks for your advice. It's helped. Hey, if you teach me to cook, maybe we could trade jobs. You're a good therapist."

"Not a chance, man. Your job doesn't tempt me in the least. I couldn't breathe in a big city, and to be honest, I think maybe you're breathing a little shallowly yourself." Jonathan chuckled. "Dude, you need a new office and a bunch of new patients."

"You could be right. In answer to your question, Teela and I are still on for tonight. I just saw—whoa!"

He ducked a little as a hummingbird zoomed toward him, seemingly at full speed, only to come to an abrupt halt six inches from his face.

Booth didn't move a muscle, other than to shoot Jonathan a wide-eyed glance.

"Be still," Jonathan whispered. "He has something to say to you."

Okay. Nice guy the chef might be, but maybe he did need a nice, cozy cell and a brand new, whitey-tightey of a straight jacket.

"Trust me." Jonathan leaned in a little closer. "Clear your mind and just…listen."

Why not? Booth fixed his gaze on the little blue-winged creature, and emptied his always-busy mind the best he could.

Nothing.

"Don't give up." Jonathan must be an empty-mind reader.

Booth forced himself to remain still and focused. Why in the world was that crazy little hummer hovering there for so long? If someone had told him about an experience like this, he wouldn't have believed them.

Trust love.

A tiny, barely audible voice in his head. So faint. Was it even real?

Unless… He sneaked a suspicious glance at Jonathan, who sat with his eyes closed, chin on his fists. If he was pranking Booth, nothing in his impassive expression gave it away. Was he praying? If so, Booth hoped those prayers included him, because hearing voices from a hummingbird could indicate he needed a whole lot of help.

God is love.

Words as old as history. *That's* the big message from the tiny messenger?

Love never fails.

As the stream of short messages continued, Booth found himself drifting into a place apart from himself. The little voice seemed not-so-faint, more like a whisper—audible, but meant for his ears only.

Not cursed. Blessed.

Not weak. Strong.

Not destined to run. Created to stand, to conquer.

Strong in love.

Strong in happiness.

Strong in Christ.

The words began to fade away. Booth struggled back from whatever place he had visited in his spirit.

The hummingbird was nowhere in sight, but Jonathan stood a few feet away, holding a glass of water. Booth accepted the offered water and discovered he was parched. Had he traveled through a desert?

"Wh—where's my little friend?"

"Flew away a moment ago. I was beginning to think you'd flown away with him."

Booth smiled. "I think I almost did." He poured more water down his throat. "Wow, I'm really thirsty."

"You've taken a spirit-walk, my friend. Not like the vision quests one hears about in the stories of my people…but not unlike them, either. You've been on a walk with God."

"A walk—a walk–" Booth stood up so fast the world spun, and he dropped back onto the swing. "Whoa."

Jonathan's big hand on his shoulder stabilized him. "A spirit-walk is a good thing. God loves to spend time with those who can hear His voice. I know you heard Him speak. I won't ask what He said, but He doesn't waste words. So heed whatever message you received."

Booth nodded. "I will. I think I'll take a, uhm…a perfectly normal, one-foot-in-front-of-the-other walk…and try to absorb what I heard."

"Good idea, man. But sit here and drink this water first. All of it." Jonathan squeezed his shoulder, then turned toward the open glass doors. "I have to get back to work."

"Hey, Jonathan…thanks, man."

"I didn't do anything." Jonathan raised both eyebrows. "I just sat here and watched God do it all."

Teela pulled a long-sleeved, pink top over Kinsley's head, smoothed it around the top of her jeans, then slipped the little one's arms into a suede vest. She grinned at the adorable picture her daughter made in the get-up. Kinsley had spotted the outfit—complete with pink boots—at one of those big roadside venues scattered along every major highway in the country. She'd absolutely had to have it, and Teela couldn't resist either. Once she donned the boots, her little Kinny Kat would be a miniature cowgirl.

Kinsley shoved back a mass of black curls and fixed a pair of curious, concerned green eyes on Teela. "Ah we *sleepin'* out thayoh, Mommy?" The little one shivered. "With the lions and tigohs and bayohs?"

Teela smiled. "We'll sleep in a bed, in a room, just like we are here, love. Not outside with the animals." She pulled the little girl in for a hug. "You know I wouldn't let anything hurt you—not ever, ever, ever!"

Kinsley laughed and struggled against the tight hold. "Mommy! I can't bweathe!"

"You can't breathe, huh?" Teela loosened her hold, but then dove in to rain kisses on her daughter's belly. "How about now, Kinny Kat?"

The tot howled with uncontrollable laughter—pudgy little hands pushing and shoving at Teela as she tried to free herself of the tickly kisses. Teela pressed one last peck on a soft, round cheek and set her free.

"Go find a pink ribbon for your hair, pumpkin, and bring me the brush. We can't have the lions seeing you like this. Why, you look like the Shagamuffin Orphan! Remember that cartoon?"

Kinsley giggled. "But I not a ohfun, 'cause I got a mommy. Wight?"

Teela swallowed the lump in her throat. "Yes, you sure do have a mommy. Not 'got,' Kinny Kat."

A frown knit the tiny brow. "But I do got one!"

Laughter spoiled any chance of further correction. She tugged on a wild strand of hair. "Go on, get that ribbon and brush. Let's get you all prettied up. We should always look our best for a concert."

For a moment, neither of them spoke as Teela smoothed and detangled her daughter's long, black hair—so like Annalise's. And those green eyes…sometimes looking at them brought on waves of intense sorrow. She'd never stop missing her friend.

"Mommy?"

"Kinny Kat?"

"I not a ohfun, 'cause I got you. But…" Her sweet voice trailed off, and she bent her head.

"What is it?" Teela turned the child to face her. A tense chill in her chest warned her of what might be coming. Still, she had to allow Kinsley her questions. "You can ask me anything."

"Okay." Her voice was still small, but she lifted her little chin and met Teela's gaze. "How come some not-ohfuns gots a daddy? I might need one o' those too, don't I?"

The brush slipped from Teela's numb fingers, and she folded the child into her arms. "Someday, perhaps, my little Kinny Kat. But I sure like having you all to myself. I love you sooo much!"

"I know, Mommy." Kinsley pulled free, picked up the brush and returned it to the vanity without being told. "But if we had a daddy, we'd have *anothoh* sooo-much love." She spread her hands wide apart and cocked her head in a move so adorable Teela teared up. "See?"

"Yep, I see. Well, we'll just have to wait until God sends us a just-right daddy, won't we?"

"Yep. 'Cept maybe He ahweady did, Mommy! How 'bout Mistoh Booth? He's just-wight."

Teela froze in the process of packing a bag for the night. She folded Kinsley's favorite blankie in silence, trying to come up with the perfect response.

The child's big eyes widened even further. They shone with a beautiful, happy light—heartbreaking to Teela, considering that joy was based so far from reality. Kinsley grinned as if she'd discovered a whole stash of forbidden chocolate. "Mistoh Booth likes me. I can tell. If he be'd my daddy, then he'd love me, like you do. Wight, Mommy?"

Never had Teela felt so far from being a "real" mother...because real mothers always know how to answer questions that put their backs against a wall. Don't they?

"Mommy?" Kinsley hadn't meant the question to be metaphorical. She expected an answer, and preferably right now. "I asked—oh! Somebody's knockin'."

She whirled toward the door, but Teela caught her arm. "What has mommy told you, sweetie?"

The child crossed both arms over her chest. "I'm not 'pos'ta ansoh the doah. I'm 'pos'ta let you do it, 'cause anybody in the whole wohld could be standin' out thayoh."

"That's right. Now put your boots on while I see who it is."

Toni stood in the hall wearing an impish smile. "So, I hear you're going to the concert, after all."

"As if you didn't know I would all along." Teela narrowed her gaze, but couldn't hold back a grin. "I'm pretty sure you know everything that happens in this place. Can you actually read the minds of your guests, Toni Littlebird?"

Toni's laughter wrapped itself around a heart still frightened by a little girl's precocious topic of conversation.

"No, I'm afraid not—and to be honest, I've had a guest or two whose minds I wouldn't have read if I could have." She twisted her lips and rolled her eyes.

Teela laughed. "I'm sure you've seen your share of that kind of person."

"Honestly, I've been beyond blessed. Most of the folks who stay at Inn the Hollow are pleasant people. God guides my choices when I accept reservations. The only mishaps take place when I'm too busy to listen before making a decision."

"I'm working on that myself, Toni. Listening isn't always easy, is it?" She smiled. "But I'm sure you didn't come up to talk about mind reading or tuning in to God's voice."

"No, but it was a nice little aside, wasn't it?" She grinned. "Actually, Jonathan asked me to have you or Booth stop by the kitchen on your way out. He's fixed a few little snacks for you to enjoy tonight while you're sitting around the fire at the 'concert.'"

"What a kind—and seriously thoughtful—thing to do! I'll have Booth come by. Would you thank Jonathan for me, please?"

"Absolutely." Toni took a step toward the stairs, then swung back. "I know the idea of entering into a romantic relationship frightens you. Just remember to keep an open mind."

"I already promised you, so I guess I have to give it my best." She stepped out to give Toni a hug. "Is Dax going to be around for Valentine's Day?"

Toni's architect fiancé lived a few hours away, on a Missouri mountain. Teela had loved the story of how they met. Apparently Dax roared into Hummingbird Hollow on a crippled Harley that stank up the air and scared away Toni's beloved hummingbirds right in the middle of her morning prayer dance. She'd been fighting mad, but when she looked into Dax's eyes, she'd known he was 'The One' God created just for her. The couple planned to be married sometime early next year.

"He's on the road right now." The woman's dark eyes shone with a beautiful lovelight. "I can't wait to see him."

"Good. I'm glad the two of you will be together."

"Me too. Now I'm going to let you finish packing." She set off once again, and again turned back. "Teela…sometimes the most amazing wisdom comes from the mouths of babes."

With no explanation of that cryptic comment, Toni waved and headed back downstairs.

Teela closed the door and slowly turned back into the room. Her gaze fell on Kinsley, who stood proudly in the little pink boots she'd put on all by herself. She widened her eyes and gave her daughter an approving smile, but her mind couldn't release Toni's comment.

From the mouths of babes…

Chapter 8

KINSLEY CHATTERED ALL THE WAY to the refuge. Booth tried to keep up—how could she flit from one topic to another...to another...at lightning speed, without a single pause? She challenged him, and he loved it.

But Teela was even quieter than usual. Something weighed on her mind. Had he done or said something to upset her?

He took her hand as they entered the main facility to check in.

"You're kind of preoccupied. Everything all right?"

Teela gave his hand a little squeeze. "Everything's fine. It's just...well, I shared some things with Toni earlier and the conversation left me feeling a little pensive, I guess."

He nodded. "Yeah, I hear you. That happens. Jonathan and I had a discussion this morning that still has me looking deep inside myself."

Her low laughter washed over him like a soothing balm. "Am I crazy, or is that place—Hummingbird Hollow as a whole, of course, but the bed and breakfast, as well—is there something a little...unusual about it?"

"You mean magical?"

"Oh, no." Her eyes widened. "Not magic. But..."

"But something that brings the word to mind, because there's a surreal quality around the inn."

"That's it. That's it exactly." She tugged on his hand, bringing him to a halt, and turned to face him. "Booth, I feel like everything I've struggled with in the past few years of my life—every doubt, or fear, or question…I've been forced to confront them in some way since I've been here. It's been painful, but therapeutic too. Healing, you know?"

"I do know. I'm right there with—"

"Mommy? Mistoh Booth?" A few feet ahead of them, Kinsley stopped and planted hands on hips. "Ah you gonna stand thayoh foh*evoh*?"

"We're coming, Kinny Kat."

They both laughed a bit self-consciously. Teela gave his fingers another little squeeze, and then gently pulled her hand free of his.

At the reception desk, the clerk grinned as he handed Booth two keys. "You know there are five cabins in this cluster?"

"Yes. We know we'll be sharing the area."

"Well, that's just it. Two of the other three were reserved—until today. Both of them cancelled just a couple hours ago." He shrugged. "Dropped reservations aren't all that unusual this time of year, but two in one day…in the same lodging section?" A confused frown knit his brow, and then the smile came back out. "Give it a couple months, and those cabins won't be empty for more than an hour between guests. But this time around, y'all have that cluster to yourselves, which means no company on the shared deck. Should be comfy and cozy with just the three of you, and—" He paused, then hiked a brow. "Everything's all set for you."

Booth smiled and nodded. "That's great! I'm sorry for the refuge, losing those reservations, but I can't say I'm disappointed to hear we'll be on our own."

"Well, y'all have a nice evenin'. Hopefully the lions will sing for you."

"We sure hope so."

They followed the map they'd been given to a group of cabins built around an octagonal deck. A large firepit beneath a gazebo-like structure dominated the center of the space. Booth could hardly wait to get a fire going and enjoy an evening under the stars with his two beautiful guests.

Teela and Kinsley both seemed excited about checking out their home for the evening. After rushing out of the car, they climbed up several steps to deck level. The five long, narrow cabins attached to the wooden deck in front, each of them on a different side of the octagon. Thick stilts braced the structures along their entire length, keeping them at a height level with the deck. Smaller, more private decks at the back of each unit overlooked the refuge grounds.

Booth walked the girls to their cabin, unlocked the door and handed the key to Teela. "Welcome to your home for the night." He nodded to the unit next to it. "I'll be in that one."

"Thank you, Booth." Teela lifted on her tiptoes to kiss his cheek. "Thank you for doing this for us."

"Oh, make no mistake, beautiful…I did this for me as much, if not more than for you."

Teela's eyebrows drew together—just a little. She smiled—just a little. "I don't understand."

He bent his head and touched his lips to her forehead. "You will."

He pushed the door wide.

Teela gave him one last, searching glance, and then led Kinsley inside.

"Ohhh!" Kinsley breathed.

"B—Booth?" Teela turned and lifted a stunned gaze to his. "Did you do—? But of course you did." She broke off and pressed her fingers to lips that visibly trembled. "It's…perfect!"

Bright rose petals covered the floor and the queen-sized bed. Artfully arranged in a tall, crystal vase, long-stemmed blooms of various colors and species graced the center of a simple pine-wood coffee table. Candlelight flickered from every surface in the room, and with the drapes pulled shut—as Booth had requested—the effect was similar to what it might have been after dark.

Each of the two bed pillows cradled a small gift—a stuffed lion with a pink-and-red polka dot bow affixed to its mane, and a fluffy red bear. The bear's arms were crossed around yet another red rose. A heart-shaped box of chocolates rested in the center of the bed.

"Happy Valentine's Day." Booth spoke quietly into the stunned silence. Even Kinsley maintained an uncharacteristic lack of chatter.

God, they're so perfect…so lovely. Both of them. Thank You for giving me this time with them.

He smiled at the mother and gave the daughter a wink. "Let's give ourselves a little time to rest, shall we? Maybe about an hour? Then we'll meet on the deck and enjoy whatever Jonathan sent for our dinner. By then, it should be getting close to time for the lions' serenade."

"Sounds perfect." Teela hauled in a breath so unsteady Booth heard the hitches. "Absolutely perfect. Like this room…like everything." Her cheeks pinked a little, but she held his gaze. "Like you, Booth. Just…perfect."

He wanted nothing more than to fold her in his arms. To tell her *she* was the perfect one. To beg her to allow him into her life, and Kinsley's.

A hundred different things he longed to say and do.

But it wasn't time. Not yet.

Bending, he touched his lips to her forehead. He meant to simply brush her skin with his lips, but found himself allowing them to linger there a little longer. He pulled away with great reluctance. "One hour, then. Rest well."

He dipped his chin like the perfect gentleman his mother had taught him to be, and strode to the door.

"M–Mommy…?"

Teela barely registered her daughter's uncertain whisper.

She had regressed to her awkward teen years through nothing more than a kiss on her forehead. For heaven's sake! When had she ever been a timid, weak-kneed, noodle-spined wimp of a woman? Never, that's when! She prided herself on being strong—totally immune to the silliness that turned some women into useless caricatures of themselves when a good-looking man happened by. And yet, here she stood, ogling the closed door as if it were made of chocolate ice cream and maraschino cherries—her favorite combination ever.

"Hmm?" Despite the self-lecture, she couldn't quite tear her gaze from the exit that had stolen Booth from her sight.

"Mommy!"

Teela's attention snapped into focus. "Sorry, Kinny Kat! What's wrong?"

"Is all this pwetty just foh us?"

Teela smiled a little sadly. Because she'd refused any man access to her life, Kinsley hadn't really been introduced to Valentine's Day. Nor did she attend day care classes or pre-school, so even that avenue of learning about the holiday had been denied her. Unable to bear having the little one out of her sight for hours at a time, Teela had taught her at home. Kinsley knew everything she might have learned in a pre-school facility, including being able to recognize and recite her numbers, all the way to one hundred. She also knew the alphabet, and rarely missed a letter when she quoted them aloud.

But Teela had failed to make her aware of this fun holiday.

"Yes, it is, sweetie. Mr. Booth did this for us, because it's Valentine's Day."

Kinsley scrunched her nose. "What's Ballentine's?"

Teela looked directly at her daughter and stressed the 'V.' "Valentine's Day, Kinny Kat. It's a special day for people to let each other know how much they care about them."

Big, green eyes rounded. Teela literally witnessed a radiant light switch on behind those pretty peepers. "Mistoh Booth cayohs about *us*?"

Uh oh. Teela pulled in a deep breath, let it out slowly. "Well, yes, darling. I suppose he does. We're all friends now, aren't we?"

"Yep." Excitement trembled her little body. "I told you he likes us, Mommy! Mistoh Booth can be owah just-wight daddy." She climbed up on the bed, grabbed the stuffed lion, and hugged it to her. "We'll be a *weoh* family."

"Why don't we talk about this later, munchkin? Right now, let's lie down and try to get a little rest before dinner. Then maybe the lions will sing for us."

"Okay." Kinsley lay back against the pillow, but popped up again just as Teela stretched out beside her. "Do you think Mistoh Booth will—?"

"Kinsley." Teela gently pressed the little one back against her pillow. "Not now. Nap time."

The child said nothing, but she let loose a sigh way too big for a body so tiny. She curled up on her side with the lion still hugged close. Her eyes closed, but she wasn't asleep. Teela could almost feel the overdose of adrenalin coursing through

Kinsley's body, and the million and one possibilities that played through her mind.

She understood, because the three-year-old wasn't the only female in the room struggling with those issues.

They both did, at last, fall asleep, but erratic, troubling images filled Teela's dreams. A car crash, a roaring lion, a knight in shining armor…riding off into the sunset. Herself in tears, watching him go. She'd rouse enough to attempt waking, only to drop into another dream segment.

She'd never been more grateful to be awakened when Kinsley tugged at her arm. "Mommy, Mommy, Mommy!" The kid was nothing if not persistent. "Somebody's at the doah. Maybe it's Mistoh Booth. Want me to let him in?"

Teela awakened in an instant.

"Thank you, sweetie, but you know better. You stay right here. I'll get the door."

She ran her fingers through her hair. Did she have pillow creases on her cheeks? Oh, well. If she did, it couldn't be helped.

Booth grinned when she peeked through a three-inch opening. "Looks like I woke you. I apologize…but dinner's laid out and ready when you girls are hungry."

Teela smiled. "Give us five minutes. I'm starving."

"I stahvin' too, Mistoh Booth," Kinsley yelled.

Booth laughed. "Well, we'll fix you right up, Sweetcake." He winked at Teela. "See you in a few."

They joined him moments later. A fire crackled in the firepit. Booth had covered two wooden tables with matching cloths. One boasted a black-and-white-striped background dotted with clusters of bright cherries and pink roses. On the other table covering, chocolate kisses and black-ribbon bows danced across a field of pale pink and bright red stripes.

Chef Jonathan's offerings, in pretty disposable dishes, covered one of the two tables. Slices of prime rib, moist chicken breasts stuffed with spinach and pepper jack cheese. Potato salad. Bacon-wrapped asparagus spears. A corn salad with cheese and chips that Teela couldn't wait to try. Sweets, too—cherry-chocolate cake, half a dozen or so squares of fudge, a fluffy pink fruit salad.

A three-armed candelabrum graced the center of the second table. In probable concession to the frequent breezes that swept the deck, small, glass votive cups, rather than taper candles, adorned each arm, and pretty flames flickered from within. Circling the bright centerpiece, black placemats held red plates and black napkins tied with white ribbon around flatware with pink acrylic handles.

"Oh, my goodness!" She shook her head, trying to take it all in. "You've set this out beautifully, Booth. And Jonathan outdid himself. Why would he send all this with us?"

"That's the kind of person he is…he and Toni both." Booth took her hand and drew her further into the gazebo. "Come. Let's eat."

"Yeah, Mommy. Let's eat!" Kinsley had already climbed up on a bench and was eyeing Jonathan's generous spread through wide green eyes. "My tummy's talking."

As if to corroborate the claim, a loud rumble from her belly followed on the heels of the statement. Kinsley slapped both hands to her mouth and giggled from behind her fingers. Booth and Teela laughed along, and then went to stand beside the little one.

"Let's pray," Booth said. "Then we can eat." He held out both hands. Teela took one. Kinsley took the other, and then held her free hand out to her mother. "Wanna hold yoah hand too, Mommy."

Standing together like that, in a little circle formed by their linked hands, Teela found herself blinking back tears. In that moment, they felt so very much like a family. But she couldn't have that. Not now. Not while Kinsley was so little.

Could she?

"Father, thank You for this chance to be together on this special day. I'm so glad you wrote Teela and Kinsley into my life's story. We appreciate this wonderful bounty of love from the folks at Inn the Hollow, and we're so very grateful for the nature around us—a special gift from You, planned for the three of us from the very moment of creation. So for the food, for nature, and for the love and friendship we all share on this day, we thank You. Amen."

He released their hands as Teela choked back tears. She raised her head to find a soft brown gaze fixed on hers, and something happened to her breath. She smiled, even as she tried to haul in air.

"Shall we?" Booth gestured toward the food table, and Teela hurried that way, grateful when her breathing leveled out without anyone noticing. She fixed a plate for Kinsley, and then one for herself, praying all the while.

Oh, Lord, please protect my heart—and my daughter's.

Because Kinsley was falling just as surely in love with Booth as was her mother. Teela could no longer deny her heart's desire. She loved this man she'd known for such a short time—and yet forever. Maybe since the beginning of time.

What if Booth simply enjoyed her company, and would disappear when all this was over? How would she go on for the rest of her life, knowing he was somewhere out there, but would never be a part of her world?

Chapter 9

WITH DINNER CLEARED AWAY, BOOTH arranged three chairs close to the fire, facing out into the darkness. Already the sun edged close to the horizon, and shadows lengthened across the ground.

"It's starting to get a little chilly," he told Teela. "You might want to bring out a blanket for Kinsley, and maybe a wrap for yourself."

"Good idea. I'll be right back."

Kinsley followed at her mother's heels, because "my lion wants to come outside too, with all the othoh lions." When they returned, she ignored her chair and stood in front of Booth. "Can I sit with you, Mistoh Booth?"

"*May* I," Teela corrected.

"Mommy, thayoh's not woom foh both of us."

Laughing, Booth hauled the child onto his lap. Teela's pink cheeks and horrified expression almost, but not quite, prevented him from teasing her. He patted the other leg and hiked a brow. "I'm sure we could make room. Mommy?"

Teela closed her eyes and shook her head. Her pretty pink blush turned bright red—but a tiny smile teased at the corners of her lips.

Kinsley erupted into gales of laughter. "She's not yoah mommy, Mistoh Booth."

"You're right, Sweetcake, she isn't." He tried to keep it light, but when his gaze met Teela's, the atmosphere thickened right along with his throat.

No trouble figuring out his own inability to take in oxygen. But why did Teela's beautiful blue eyes reflect enough panic to freeze a family of deer on a Los Angeles freeway? Was she so afraid he'd fall in love with her and ruin their new, naturally developing friendship?

Booth fought back panic of his own. *Easy, dude. She's like a skittish mare. No sudden movements, and no overstepping her comfort zone…not until she loses that inclination to run.*

Kinsley remained uncharacteristically quiet during the silent exchange between the two adults.

The lions did not.

Just when Booth thought his mouth would betray him and say the wrong words at the wrong time, a deep chuffing sound, clearly emanating from the throat of a rather large animal, filled the night air. An echo of chuffs followed—the first in a rain of not-quite-roars.

Kinsley clutched his shirt with all ten fingers. "What was that?" she whispered.

Booth cuddled her closer. "That was the intro to our concert. No need to be afraid, Sweetcake."

She nodded, but her tiny body trembled a bit against his torso. Instinct kicked in, and he found himself rubbing little circles on her back, aching to calm her fears.

Teela met his gaze and slammed him with the most gorgeous, radiant smile. No human creature should possess that kind of smile. It wasn't fair to other human creatures. Booth chuffed a little himself, and sent up a silent thanks that he'd been seated when she loosed that weapon on him. Otherwise, he would most likely have fallen on his rear and taken Kinsley along with him.

After that first round of not-quite-melodic chuffs, the concert began in earnest. The lions roared, but not as one would expect from an angry or threatened creature. The softer sound—especially with many lion voices providing a rough harmony—became, almost literally, a song.

Booth closed his eyes for a moment, absorbing the sound. Vocalized by creatures far closer to nature and God than he would ever be, the unusual song gripped his heart and emotions in a way he'd not experienced in any formal church service or professional music concert. This wasn't just any song, sung by just any singer. This was a melody so deeply ingrained in nature that it became almost a call of the 'wild'—only, for Booth, it was a draw toward his Maker, his Creator, the One who'd been his best Friend as a youth. The God who was showing Himself still real in Booth's life even now…at Inn the Hollow, with Teela, in his discussions with Chef Jonathan.

Were the lions joining their voices in a song of praise?

Remembering Teela's dance as she prayed in Toni's garden, Booth risked another glance in her direction. Tears streaked her cheeks. No surprise there. He barely held them back himself.

As if she felt his gaze, Teela lifted tear-misted blue eyes to meet his. "I'm sorry, I—" She slid to the edge of her seat in a graceful movement that almost made it seem she simply 'blinked' from one position to the next. "Do you mind if I praise with them?"

Mind? He'd been blessed with free admission to the greatest show on earth.

"Please, love…dance."

She shot him a startled glance, even as she rose in a single, fluid motion and moved around the firepit to an open space between the fire and the deck's edge.

Booth emitted a rueful sigh. She hadn't asked permission to dance…only to praise. He knew she praised God in dance only because he'd witnessed her and Toni in the garden, each of them offering their own brand of praise in two equally stunning dance styles.

She might ask about his verbal *faux pas* later, but for now, Teela's entire body and mind seemed set on joining the lions' worship session.

Having almost forgotten he held a child in his arms, Booth had a moment of startled reaction when Kinsley snuggled closer. He glanced down to find her gaze fixed on her mother. But she said nothing—quite surprising, considering her normal tendency to be a delightful chatterbox.

He tightened his hold around her, just enough to make her feel secure, and then returned his attention to the lovely woman pouring her heart out to God in a beautiful, graceful dance.

Teela bent and swayed, twisted and turned, leapt and landed on feet that moved in constant, joyful grace and rhythm. Somehow, as she focused increasingly inward—no. Booth rethought the word. As she became completely *Heavenward*-focused, the lions' voices also took on a more rhythmic feel, so in tune with one another that their song became unmistakably harmonic. Each soft, deep roar blended together, almost as if they spoke in one deep, soul-shaking voice.

The concert continued for close to half an hour. Teela slowed her twirling movements in direct correlation to the lions' winding down of chuffing, roaring harmony. When it ended, she went limp on the deck floor. Booth sat forward, certain she'd fallen. But, no. She'd stretched both arms out in front of her head as it touched the deck floor, and simply rested there a moment…perhaps a winding-down of her own.

Then she stood and walked toward him, a glorious smile lighting her face.

"I can never thank you enough for tonight, Booth. Until someone hears something like this for themselves, they can never really understand what it's like. There aren't words enough in any language to describe it. I know I couldn't tell anyone exactly what it was like. Could you?"

"No. Never." Booth left it at that, even though he referred to far more than the amazing lion-choir.

Her head tilted, and she knelt in front of him. "My little munchkin didn't last through the performance. Here, I'll take her in."

Booth shook his head. "I'll carry her. You lead the way."

She hesitated, but then stood and headed for her cabin. Inside, she pulled back the covers on one side of the double bed.

Booth bent low and gently positioned the child with her head on the pillow. Long hair fell over her face. He lifted it away with one finger, and then stroked that same digit gently down her cheek. A tiny smile curved her lips, and Booth's heart fell at her feet.

Boy, was he ever a goner! This sweet child and her mother owned his whole heart.

Teela stepped close and tucked the little stuffed lion into Kinsley's arms. She must have picked it up off the deck floor, where it had fallen when the little one dropped off to sleep.

"There," Teela whispered. "She'll be out for the night now."

She raised up and fixed an inquisitive gaze on Booth. "Are you tired, or are you up to a fireside chat?"

Booth offered her his arm. "Come with me, beautiful. Let's talk."

Teela scooted her chair closer to Booth's, so they could speak in quieter tones, although she wasn't sure she could carry on a conversation that made any kind of sense.

She'd never experienced the kind of God-touch that happened as she danced to the lions' song. Something about the whole setting touched her on a deep, almost primitive level, and took her to a spiritual high place she'd never before attained. Being within the sanctuary grounds lent a sort of Garden-of-Eden effect. The lions' caroling, coming as it did from the voices of creatures God made on the same day He breathed life into mankind, also contributed to her total loss of self and self-consciousness as she praised God with her entire being.

When at last she rose from the deck where she'd wilted in total surrender at the end of her prayer-dance, her gaze fell immediately on Booth.

Booth…cradling her daughter in his arms like something he treasured.

Booth…watching her as she returned to his side, with something in his gaze that weakened her knees and turned her prided strength into mush.

Then he'd deposited Kinsley on her bed with such gentle care, as if he'd been putting children down for the night forever. Everything about the man pulled and tugged at her heart. But with that final, unexpected stroke of his finger down her daughter's cheek…that's when Teela knew without a doubt that her heart belonged to Booth Meadows.

But could she release her fervent self-promise to make Annalise's child the total focus of her life until such time as Kinsley didn't need her anymore?

"Tell me about your life in Sugar Land, Teela. What do you do there?"

"A bit of everything." Mundane conversation. Good…she

could use that. Otherwise she might spill her feelings all over Booth, uninvited and unwanted. "I teach dance for a living, and donate time to the church as a praise dance team leader."

"And you're the perfect mother to an active, precocious, amazing little girl."

"Well, I don't know about 'perfect.' But mothering Kinsley is a pleasure, pure and simple."

"Still. It adds to your load, which you seem to handle with no problem at all."

"Oh, trust me. I have my moments." She raised her head and met his somber gaze. "But I promised myself when Annalise died that I would dedicate myself entirely to her child. Until Kinsley doesn't need me anymore, I have to be there for her all the way, in every way."

"Is that why you've never married?"

"It's the biggest reason. I can't imagine taking care of a husband in addition to what I already do."

He nodded, and then a slow smile spread over his face and warmed his eyes. "You're looking at this all wrong, you know."

"Is that so?" She stiffened a little. Was he really going to criticize her thought process?

"In a real marriage—a good marriage—loads aren't made heavier. They're shared, and thereby lightened. You and your husband...you'd take care of each other, and you'd both be there for Kinsley. The best of all worlds, right?"

She sat silent for a long time. So simply stated, and yet such a powerful truth. Why hadn't she figured it out for herself?

I tried to figure out the biggest responsibility of my life on my own. God could have shown me how to do it right, from the very beginning. I just didn't ask.

Well, it wasn't too late. She hoped.

"Those may be the wisest words I've heard in a while,

Booth. But what about you? What do you do? For that matter, where do you live? I know absolutely nothing about you."

That's true. You don't know that my bloodline runs thick with deadbeat dads. You don't know that I'm scared to death I'll be like those men. Meadows men run...they don't stick around.

As if in answer to his thoughts, a blast of powerful wind hit him in the chest and he grabbed the arms of his chair, certain he and it would fall backward. Yet his frantic glance at Teela revealed a woman sitting at ease in her chair smiling, relaxed...and not a breath of movement mussed her hair.

The voice that followed blew in the wind, and it was not a whisper. Yet, once again, Teela seemed totally unaware. She sat with an expectant expression, awaiting a reply he was unable to give while held in the grip of a tornado-force wind and a voice from nowhere and everywhere.

Not cursed. Blessed.

Not weak. Strong.

Not destined to run. Created to stand, to conquer.

Strong in love.

Strong in happiness.

Strong in Christ.

He pulled in a breath that hurt his chest and then scratched his throat. Shame burned hot in his cheeks. He'd always been a fast learner. God shouldn't have to keep reminding him again and again.

I get it, Lord. I'm not cursed. You have blessed me with a new outlook and, hopefully, a new life. I don't have to follow in my father's and grandfathers' footsteps, because You're with me—You're in me—and that makes me strong...in You. Not weak. I won't run from the blessings You give me. Not now, not ever.

The wind that apparently blew only on him stopped in a

blink.

"Booth?" Teela finally showed a reaction to his long pause. "Are you okay? You look a little pale."

"I'm, uh…" He drew a couple of deep breaths and then smiled, determined not to wreck the evening. "I'm good. Actually, never better."

"Good, then…tell me about Booth Meadows."

He shrugged. "Not a lot to tell. I live in Hollywood, and work as a counselor to the rich and famous of that self-focused city."

"Ouch. You don't sound too excited about it."

"To be honest, I'm here in Arkansas because I'm more than a little disenchanted with the whole Hollywood scene. I became a counselor to help people navigate genuine issues. Most of my clients think they need counseling, but they're really just trying to fill a void in their lives—one their money and power can't fill, and neither can I." He sighed. "I'm used up, Teela. Fed up, worn down and burnt out. I don't know if I'll ever be any good at my job anymore."

"Of course you will. Don't you see, Booth? You're just playing for the wrong crowd."

He cocked his head, a little frown drawing his dark eyebrows together. "Meaning?"

"Maybe the Hollywood crowd isn't your intended clientele. Have you taken time to pray about that?"

"No." He rested a warm gaze on her. "But this sounds a lot like what Jonathan said to me this morning. I promise I will pray about it."

"Good. There are lots of other places for professionals. My own little suburb of Sugar Land has been crying for another good counselor for a long time." She grinned. "Just sayin'."

He shook his head. "I have to confess, I haven't been much of one for prayer in recent years. It's only since I arrived at

Hummingbird Hollow that I've found my way back to God." He drew a deep breath and then locked his gaze onto hers. "And that's because I was an unintentional witness to your early-morning dance—and Toni's—in the gardens a few days back."

"You saw that? Booth, I came upon Toni dancing, and simply couldn't resist praising along with her." She smiled and reached over to lay a hand atop his. "It appears we were both 'unintentional witnesses' that morning."

"I guess so. But you only witnessed Toni. I saw both of you, and it was…" He paused, and a muscle in his jaw flexed. "Powerful. Incredibly heart-stirring. Intensely moving. I prayed that morning for the first time in many years. Since then, I find myself carrying on an almost constant conversation with God. About little things and big ones. I'm rebuilding the relationship with Christ that I sacrificed to my career a long time ago."

"Oh, Booth! I'm thrilled that I could be even a small part of that reunion."

She smiled, and then reclaimed her hand. She'd helped Booth find his way back to God. The knowledge humbled her, and she bowed her head to breathe a prayer of thanks.

"Teela?" Booth's hand covered hers. He seemed to need that contact, while it all but drove her out of her mind. "Are you okay?"

She drew a deep breath and smiled. "Better than okay. How can I ever thank you enough for this incredible evening?"

"Just having the two of you here with me would be enough. But then you gave me the incredible gift of watching you dance along with the lion's song. I'm the one who should be asking…how can I thank you?"

She turned in her chair to face him more fully. "Then we're both happy. That's good. But I want to thank you, too, for being so sweet with my little girl. Not everyone has your kind of affinity for children."

He chuckled. "I didn't know I did. And to be honest, I'm not sure I do—except, with Kinsley, it's different. It's almost like she's…well, like she's mine."

"I see that, and it kind of scares me. Because she feels that way too, and I'll have to deal with her questions and tears when she realizes you're gone and she's unlikely to ever see you again."

"It doesn't have to be like that, you know." Booth leaned forward in his chair. "Why does her heart need to break? Why does mine?"

Chapter 10

"Y—YOURS?" THE TREMBLE IN HER voice matched the tremor that ran through Booth's entire body.

"Mine. I love you, Teela. I love that little girl. Up until now, my life has been a wasteland. Empty and meaningless. But you…you've filled my heart so completely, I can't even fathom my world without you in it."

"Booth…"

In the light from the nearby fire, the moisture that brimmed in her eyes wasn't hard to notice.

"Don't. Don't say anything yet." He rushed to save the moment. "Think about it, please. I know you feel *something* for me. Your beautiful eyes tell me you do—or maybe that's wishful thinking on my part. But sweetheart, we could do this. We could build a life together."

"I know we could."

"Just think about—wait…what? Wh—what did you say?"

She laughed softly. "I said I know we could…build a life together. I love you, Booth. I thought I couldn't, because I promised myself Kinsley would be my whole world as long as she needs me, but now…"

"Yes?" Didn't she know this wasn't the time for lengthy pauses? His heart couldn't take them.

"Now I know I can't be everything I need to be to Kinsley

until I myself am complete. And I'm not complete—not without you."

He rose slowly from his chair and held out a hand. Teela placed hers in it and he tugged her gently upward and into his arms.

"You *love* me?" Dare he believe he wasn't dreaming?

"With everything I am."

"Whew!" He hauled her against his chest. "What did I ever do to deserve you?"

Teela snuggled against him and lifted her face to look into his eyes. "Since when do we ever deserve God's gifts?"

Wow! What a concept.

He nodded. "A gift. A Valentine's Day gift from God. That's what you are, my beautiful, dancing darling. The greatest gift of my life." He lowered his face and brushed his lips across hers—just the barest whisper of a kiss. "Are you sure, Teela? I can't bear to think you're mine and then lose you."

"Should you ever lose me, it won't be because I've changed my mind. All I can do is promise you all of me, for all my life. The rest is up to God."

"I'm still learning to trust like that, but I know you're right…and I'm getting there." He pulled her closer, and a smile tugged at his lips. "I'd like to kiss you now, Teela Vincent. Really kiss you."

She laughed and slid her arms up and around his neck. "I thought you were never going to get around to that, Booth Meadows."

"I've been waiting my whole life for you, my love. I will kiss you every day—every hour, if possible—for the rest of it."

He dipped his head then and made good on his promise with a kiss that filled all the lonely nights of his past. He prayed it did the same for her, laying to waste all the years of thinking she'd be alone for the rest of her life.

Moments later, from somewhere in the expanse of nature beyond, a low, rumbling *chuff* pulled them back to reality.

Booth lifted his lips from hers and they both hurried to the edge of the deck. In the distance, the silhouette of a lone lion stood tall and proud atop a large rock. His massive, maned head turned toward them in the moonlight. One last *chuff*, and then the animal sprang from the boulder in a graceful leap and sauntered off into the night.

Teela hauled in a deep breath, and Booth followed suit when she pressed herself close to his side. "That was like an 'amen' to this incredible evening."

"I think it was an 'amen' to us—our being together."

She leaned her head against his shoulder and he felt her smile. "Amen."

Back at Hummingbird Hollow the next day, Booth leaned against his car door with Teela folded in his arms. His stomach clenched and churned. How could he stand to leave her? But with his reservation at Inn the Hollow used up, he had to move on.

Not home. Not yet, anyway...maybe never. But somewhere.

Teela and Kinsley planned to leave tomorrow, headed into the next leg of their road trip. Oh, how he'd love to travel with them! But he hesitated to invite himself. Crowding Teela might be a bad idea.

Sighing, he touched his lips to her forehead. She snuggled against his chest and wrapped her arms around his waist.

"Don't go," she pleaded.

Booth chuckled. "I can't stay here forever, love. My reservation is over, and Toni is most likely expecting other guests."

She lifted her face to look at him. The mischievous smile on her lips turned his emotions inside out.

"She told me that you weren't here for the last night of your reservation, so if you want to stay one more night, you're welcome to do so. Your room isn't booked until tomorrow night. So stay, please?" She traced the shape of his lips with her finger. "We said we'd give 'us' a chance. That'll be hard to do with you in California and me who knows where…and then back home in Sugar Land. Come with Kinsley and me, Booth! This is our chance to dance, to find out who we are together."

Booth folded her in his arms. He couldn't resist one long, possessive kiss before giving his answer. "Of course I'll come, love—especially if you're dancing. Just promise me one thing…"

"Anything." Her breathy voice would have broken his resistance to bits, if he'd had any in the first place.

"Save a dance for me."

"Every dance, Booth. Every step of every dance is yours, through however many tomorrows we are given."

Booth answered with a kiss. A real kiss. One that promised lots of tomorrows…and a lifetime of dances.

Dear Reader,

Thank you for reading *Like a Dance*! Your time is valuable, and I'm so honored you chose to read one of my stories. If you enjoyed it (and I hope you did!), please consider talking it up with your friends and sharing your thoughts on Amazon. Positive reviews, even just a couple of sentences, help other readers discover new-to-them authors and promote clean, quality fiction. Again, thank you so much. Happy reading!

Spinach and Pepper Jack - Stuffed Chicken Breasts

4 boneless, skinless chicken breasts
8 oz frozen spinach (thawed and well-drained)
Pepper Jack cheese, sliced thin and halved
2 T bread crumbs
Salt to taste
Pepper to taste

1. Preheat oven to 350°
2. Make width-wise incisions into chicken, about ½ inch apart. Do not cut all the way through the breast.
3. Stuff each incision with 2 oz spinach and 1 piece (half slice) of pepper jack
4. Salt and pepper to taste
5. Sprinkle bread crumbs over stuffed chicken
6. Place each breast on an individual, lightly greased slice of tin foil, and "bowl" the foil around it to contain juices and keep breasts moist. Place in large baking dish (13 x 9 works well)
7. Bake for 30 minutes or until chicken is thoroughly cooked. Remove from tin foil and serve.

Note: For a Cajun flare, combine the bread crumbs with 1 T Cajun seasoning before sprinkling over chicken breasts. Yum!

We serve this dish with rice pilaf or a simple pasta (mac 'n cheese, or a nice, creamy penne)

Enjoy this

Sneak Peek

into

Hummingbird Kisses

(Hummingbird Hollow, #1)

1

"GOOD MORNING, LITTLE ONE." TONI Littlebird spoke softly to the tiny creature perched on her outstretched hand. As always, a thrill of pleasure coursed through her blood at the simple but exhilarating contact. "Aren't you a beauty!"

The hummingbird cocked his head one way and then the other. When another hummer landed on Toni's opposite shoulder, his wings fluttered with the lightning speed typical of his species but then settled again without further protest.

Toni laughed—a gentle purr of delight that wouldn't frighten her little feathered friends.

"That's right…be nice. I know you guys like to guard your turf, but here in the hollow, you're on my territory. You're all welcome, and I'll not have you running each other off."

As if they understood every word, the hummers seemed content to allow each other a bit of space. Within moments, small jewel-toned birds lined both of Toni's arms and shoulders. A couple of them nestled into the palms of her hands.

She continued a stream of quiet conversation...a variation of the same words she spoke to her tiny visitors every day. A few she addressed by names she'd given them, though she could never explain how she recognized those few hummingbirds apart from the others.

"I must go inside, my sweet darlings. The Coming Up Valentines Dinner and Dance is tonight, so there's a lot to be done today. Will you all be on your best behavior for my guests, please? Diamond, you keep the peace out here, OK? Sapphire will help, won't you, sweetness?"

She gently lifted her arms and, as a matter of routine, began to turn in gentle, swaying circles, honoring her hummingbirds in what she thought of as a ritual "see you later" dance. Eyes closed, she drank in the warmth of the sun on her face and the near-zero weight of the birds lining her arms and riding her shoulders. Her favorite part of every morning was this time spent with the lovely, fascinating birds who so inexplicably loved the hollow and her gardens as much as she did.

But this time her dance wasn't destined for the customary slow-to-a-standstill finale—the gentle farewell to the birds, who always remained in place as she danced, never lifting off to soar away until she'd blown kisses and spoken soft, loving words of goodbye.

Instead, an ugly roar split the air. Distant at first, it became more abrasive and disruptive with every moment. Loud music accompanied the discordant, mechanical growl. As the noisy intrusion reached a decibel of such intensity that Toni's ears ached, the tiny birds on her arms and shoulders first began to tremble—despite her quiet reassurances—then lifted and darted away, almost as one.

A sudden, overwhelming chemical smell filled the air.

Toni's hands flew to her face but covering her nose didn't reduce the unpleasant odor. The distinct stench of oil and gas billowed over and around the house in a noxious cloud. Never had Hummingbird Hollow been subject to such odorous and ear-crunching company!

Anger bordering on outrage drove Toni toward the inn, set on giving a proper tongue-lashing to whomever was responsible for the rude intrusion on the peace and quiet of the hollow…but mostly on her treasured morning interlude with her tiny, winged friends.

She rushed through the kitchen, ignoring the wide-eyed, questioning glances of the kitchen staff. On she went, past a formal dining room and through the huge common room with its impressive rock fireplace. Today she didn't give the striking floor-to-ceiling feature a fleeting glance.

An over-sized entrance served as the sign-in space for her bed and breakfast, Inn the Hollow. She flew through the archway and zoomed across the floor toward the door, which opened just as she reached it. Toni catapulted into a big, broad, unyielding chest covered in black leather.

"Oh!" She bounced backward but was saved the indignity of falling on her backside when a strong arm circled her waist and pulled her against the leather-covered chest once again.

"Whoa! Can't have you falling for me like that." Amusement lent pleasant undertones to a deep voice that rumbled like silent thunder in the chest against which Toni's body was pinned. For an inexplicable moment, she found herself longing to simply stay there, held in those strong arms, with the smell of male sweat and warm leather filling her senses.

She gasped and pushed herself away. The contact suddenly felt disturbingly intimate.

"Don't flatter yourself. You were in my way, and besides,

I'm pretty sure you're the one who interrupted my morning meditation and frightened my friends away."

Despite her own respectable five-foot, eight-inch frame, Toni found she needed to look up to make eye contact. Right now, she could see nothing but that broad, leather-covered chest. The fact that she was reluctant to look elsewhere stoked the fire of anger already lit within her. She jerked her traitorous gaze upward, and found, instead of a neck, a long, rather unkempt, dark blonde beard.

Ugh. Facial hair. She'd never found it attractive—probably something to do with her Native American ancestry—so she continued her visual journey but slammed on mental brakes in the next instant. Between the beard and mustache that surrounded them, an amused half smile claimed full, well-defined lips, the lower of which was fuller and even more sensual than the upper. Fascinated, Toni found herself reluctant to look away—until those perfect lips twitched further upward in obvious amusement.

Allowing her gaze to move on past an impossibly straight nose, Toni bit back a gasp when she met a pair of startling blue-green eyes. Kind, gentle, fun-loving eyes that reached out and touched her soul. They were *the* eyes. The ones she'd known, without being able to describe, would someday turn her world upside down. Eyes that belonged to *him*—the man God had created just for her. The man she'd always said she'd know when she looked into his eyes.

This man...whoever he was.

Her heart sank. This man...who'd interrupted the peaceful tranquility she so loved about Hummingbird Hollow. This man...who boasted long, untended, dark golden-brown strands—on his chin, on his head, and hanging several inches down his back.

This man, whose name she didn't yet know, and whose

entrance into her life had been anything but romantic, was God's choice of a life partner for LiTonya Littlebird, better known as Toni, who owned and operated Hummingbird Hollow's bed and breakfast, Inn the Hollow.

Toni sighed. *God never makes a mistake. His choice is always right.* Things she'd been taught all her life and believed with all her heart. Still, in this telling moment, she couldn't help but wonder. Surely, Lord, you didn't intend to send me this…this barbarian!

Having smoothed her top and brushed off her slacks with slow movements and trembling fingers, she lifted her gaze, determined to appear strong and, most importantly, unshaken by the powerful revelation. With her anger tamped a mere hair by shock, Toni crossed her arms and took a backward step away from the mountainous man in her doorway.

"Well, whatever horse you rode in on needs to be given a proper burial. It's stinking up my hollow. Tell me what I can do for you, so you can get that thing out of here. I can only hope the stench clears before my guests arrive tonight."

Right out of an Indian fairy tale!

Despite the twin circles of outrage on the woman's cheeks, Dax Hendrick found it quite impossible to remove his gaze from her face. She epitomized beauty. Pure, undefiled, completely natural beauty. This creature, whom he'd held in the circle of his own arms, was the stuff of every man's most creative imagination.

Perfection. He'd found perfection, embodied in this raven-haired woman who could only be of Native American descent. The high cheekbones and blue-black hair bespoke her heritage.

But what of those eyes? Not black, but not brown either. Not green. Somewhere between the three colors, and nearly translucent, her gaze held the power to hypnotize and mesmerize. Dax fought the urge to stare into them as if searching for the meaning of life.

"Well?" She snapped her fingers a few inches from his nose. "Are you going to tell me your name, and why you've disturbed the peace of Hummingbird Hollow? I'll have to pray a million prayers to cleanse the stink from my home."

"A million? That's a bit of an exaggeration, don't you think? Do your gods truly require such an over-abundance of pleading before they answer? Because, if so, I can introduce you to—"

"I serve Jesus Christ, stranger, and you are correct—I misspoke. He answers my every sincere prayer, and there is no need to repeat my sincere petitions again." Those lovely, indescribable eyes glittered across the counter behind which she'd hidden her graceful form. "I guess I'm a little shaken by your thunderous entrance. Between the blaring cacophony you probably call music, and the roar of your engine, I fear my beloved hummingbirds will never make another appearance in this hollow."

Dax opened his mouth, but she didn't give him a chance to speak.

"If you'll tell me how I can help you get back on the road, I'll be happy—more than happy—to get you on your way."

He couldn't take his eyes off the beautiful proprietress, whose blood clearly ran about as warm as a rattlesnake's. How was it even possible for such astounding beauty to exist in the same vessel with a vitriolic personality of this degree?

Maybe he'd made a mistake, and this big, haphazardly designed residence wasn't the one he'd seen with disturbing regularity in recent meditative moments. Maybe another, similar hollow existed somewhere in Arkansas, and he'd simply made a mistake. Surely this one, though downright beautiful, couldn't be the same peaceful little vale he'd seen in every prayer picture he'd been shown for the past six months.

Except it was, and he knew it.

"Well?" The woman drummed her fingernails—clean and well-shaped, but not fake in any way—on the countertop. "I really don't have all day, sir." When she spoke again, uncertainty softened the edges of her previously acerbic tone. "Can I help you in some way?"

Dax stood for a moment longer, studying the woman…and his surroundings, which were tastefully decorated and receptive, despite the absence of professional planning and design. Walls jutted off from one another in a sad lack of symmetry. Corners didn't always meet in perfect harmony, which grated Dax's nerves and left him vaguely nauseated. Whoever had built this structure hadn't known a thing about architecture. And yet someone—probably the breathtaking lady who stood frowning at him across the counter—had managed to make it warm, welcoming, and pleasing to the casual eye.

Now if only he possessed such a thing. The only way he knew to look at any structure with walls was purely professional, always assessing the good points and bad ones.

He pulled in a deep breath and held it a few seconds. When he felt certain he could respond with any kind of grace, he smiled. The woman was like a stunning desert cactus—lovely to the eye, but painful to the touch.

"Yes, ma'am. I'd like to claim my reservation, if you don't mind."

A soft gasp and a slight widening of the eyes gave away her surprise. "You…have a reservation? Here? At Inn the Hollow?"

At his nod, she ran a finger down one of the pages in an open registry on the counter. At last, she raised her gaze—which bordered on repentant—to his.

"Are you Dax Hendrick?"

"I am."

"And I—" She broke off and nibbled at her lip. A small storm brewed in her eyes. "I apologize."

Dax grinned, impressed with the woman's strong will and easy grace. "Then all is forgiven?"

Her level gaze held a world of...something. Something Dax found himself eager to explore.

"I wouldn't go that far, Mr. Hendrick. My hollow still smells like oil and gas, and my sweet hummingbirds are still hiding out somewhere in the trees. I can only pray they might return tomorrow." She laid a pen on the counter. "I'm Toni Littlebird. Welcome to my home. If you'll just sign the registry, sir. Will you be paying with cash or credit card?"

And just like that, she set the basis for their relationship. Professional. Honest to a fault. Well, he could handle that.

Except...those eyes of hers made him want to scratch "professional" off the list, and dive head first into "personal."

Oh, well. One couldn't have it all. Right now, he had a sick Harley to care for, and according to this woman, his ailing baby stank. So he had a little clean-up to do.

Dax carried his one duffel bag inside and checked out his room—clean, neat, and decorated with an eye to the owner's heritage. A large dreamcatcher hung over the bed. On the opposite wall, a colorful blanket, woven in a design that screamed Native American. A similar one draped the foot of the bed, and a luxurious fur rug added warmth and interest to the floor. He nodded once. This would do.

Yet his trained eye caught the slight imperfections—walls that weren't quite even, a telltale give in the floor due to discrepancies in measurement, or perhaps craftsmanship. Without meaning to do so, he noticed space-saving measures that had been overlooked. Then again, at the time this place was built, not a lot of consideration had been given to such things.

At the thought, a chuckle rumbled from between his lips. Who knew when it had been built? Without even searching out the structure's history, he knew that it was an architectural mutt—it had grown a wing here and a room there, over a good many years and quite a few owners, with little thought to aesthetics or proper building techniques. Various sections of the home spread every which direction from the central core. The result provided more living space—clearly the original intent—but brought no dynamics into play. Heating and cooling had to be major costs, given all the randomly added space. He doubted the place had central air and heat. Insulation? Certainly not a given. With all the faulty construction quirks, how could his hostess even afford to keep the doors open?

Not his problem. He tossed his duffel into a small closet, took a moment to splash water in his face and wash his hands, then headed back downstairs. He'd take a quick walk to stretch his legs, and maybe find some out-of-the-way place where he could hide his ugly, stinky Harley until he got it back in shape.

About Delia

Writing Heaven's touch into earthly tales, **Delia Latham** puts her characters through the fire of earthly trials to bring them out victorious by the hand of God, His heavenly messengers, and good, old-fashioned love. You'll always find a touch of the divine in her tales of sweet romance.

Delia and her husband Johnny live in East Texas, where their pampered Pomeranian, Kona, kindly allows them to share her home. The author enjoys multiple life roles as wife, mother, grandmother, sister and friend, but above all, she loves being a princess daughter to the King of kings. She admits to a lifelong, mostly unbattled Dr. Pepper addiction, and loves hearing from her readers.

delia@delialatham.net

amazon.com/author/delialatham

facebook.com/delialatham

twitter.com/delialatham

More Titles by

Delia Latham

Hummingbird Hollow
Hummingbird Kisses (#1)
Never the Twain (#2)

Paradise Pines
Winter Wonders (#4)
Autumn Falls (#3)
Summer Dreams (#2)
Spring Raine (#1)

Heart's Haven Novellas
Jewels for the Kingdom
Lexi's Heart
Love in the WINGS
A Cowboy Christmas
(Co-authored with Tanya Stowe)
Oh, Baby!

Pure Amore
A Christmas Beau
At First Sight
Jingle Belle

Love at Christmas Inn: Collection 1
Bells on Her Toes
Love at Christmas Inn: Collection 2
The Button Box

Smoky Mountain Christmas
Do You See What I See?
(See Amazon listing for titles
in this collection by other authors)

Solomon's Gate
Destiny's Dream (Book One)
Kylie's Kiss (Book Two)
Gypsy's Game (Book Three)
Lea's Gift (Bonus story, co-authored with Tanya Stowe)

Stand-alone Titles
The First Noelle
Treehouse (Short Story)
Yesterday's Promise
Goldeneyes

Children's Picture Book
Mine!

The following anthologies/collections contain
works/quotes by this author: